DARK OR BITTER

A collection of short stories

By

T.G. Hyde

Copyright © T G Hyde 2021
Cover design by AE Davies
Edited and Published by
© AC Publishing

This edition published in April 2022

T.G. Hyde has asserted his right under the Copyright, Designs & Patents Act 1988, to be identified as the author of this work.

All rights reserved. No part of this publication may be reproduced, stored in a retrieval system, or transmitted, in any form or by any means without the prior written permission of the author, nor be otherwise circulated in any form of binding or cover other than in which it is published and without a similar condition being imposed on the subsequent purchaser.

AC Publishing
18 Seaview Terrace
Swansea
SA1 6FE

I am dedicating this book to my parents, without whose unwavering support and encouragement I would not have achieved this.

Originally from Merthyr Tydfil, Glenn Hyde has been based in Swansea for around fifteen years. As a proud Welshman, he has had some of his fictional works published in Anglo-Welsh anthologies, which he finds particularly gratifying.

Glenn has been inspired by writers such as Guy De Maupassant, Ray Bradbury, Emile Zola and others, particularly by their ability to put so much into relatively few pages. Readers may also recognise the influence of TV shows such as The Twilight zone and Black Mirror.

In this collection, TG Hyde has put together six unconnected and seemingly disconnected stories. Be prepared for the unexpected, the surprising and the bewildering. From dark and gloomy to humorous and quirky, one thing links them – his unwavering awareness of the human condition in its many and varied forms. No judging, no moralising. Just observing, accepting. and sometimes imagining.

CONTENTS

	Page
CALL KATIE	9
STICKS AND STONES	45
THE BEGGAR	61
BALL OF CONFUSION	121
PIANO MAN	129
BONNIE WOULD UNDERSTAND	165

CALL KATIE

After enduring what seemed like an endless journey on public transport during rush hour, Katie Sutton finally arrived home. She was carrying a package, a small box. A present, gift wrapped in plain light blue paper.

'Dan, Dan.....you OK? I'm home.', she called from the small hallway of the apartment. Katie didn't expect an answer from her fiancé; nor for that matter did she get annoyed when she found him still in bed at four o'clock on this mild spring afternoon.

'I'm not going to start on at you, but you're not helping yourself are you?' she said.

'Tired, still tired Kate', Dan replied. He was sat up in bed dressed in an old pair of shorts and a T-shirt. The blinds were open, but the window was closed. The air was stale, and Dan looked exhausted. He got up and opened the window while Katie headed out to the kitchen.

'Come on, I'll make some coffee. I don't know about you, but I really need one.'

Dan followed her out slowly.

'Just a glass of water for me please. I'd better not have any caffeine, it feels like there's a cinder block on the top of my head. It's like cold turkey, coming off these meds. I'm not sure if I'm ready yet.' He noticed the package next to Katie's bag on the worktop.

'Is that for me?'

'Now who else would it be for, silly?' Katie answered. Dan managed a smile.

'Well, if it's an alarm clock, it's going through the window!'

'Hey, don't be cheeky! It sounds like someone's starting to come alive though. There, open it.' Katie passed him his present.

'A new phone ... thanks,' he mumbled as he tore off the wrapping paper. 'Another new phone I might add. That's the second in a matter of months. I've lost count of how many you've got me since you switched jobs. I don't want to sound ungrateful but, you know...'

'You know what Dan?' snapped Katie. 'They're free, and the old ones have been recycled. Just one of the perks of working for an advertising company. You make contacts in my occupation. I have contacts in big Tech firms. Anyway, the reason I got you this, is because I hope....sorry, I think

… that it will help you. It has some groundbreaking software. Tracking systems, reminders and ...'

Dan threw the unopened box onto the table. 'Tracking systems? I've had a bit of a relapse. It's nervous exhaustion, I haven't got amnesia!'

'Please keep calm. I'm just trying to help'.

'I know you are. I'm sorry.' Dan picked the box up and took the phone out. 'It's...um...small, really small'.

'Come on, show a little enthusiasm. I mean, it's one thing when you wouldn't allow a new generation Virtual Assistant in here, but go with me on this.'

'Those...quasi-robot things just intrude on your privacy. You remember that news report from the UK a few years back? Jesus, every one of those corporations had their workers listening back to users' commands and queries.'

'That was to improve the quality of speech recognition. They stopped that,' Katie stated confidently as she poured herself a coffee.

'I don't care. It's not right.' Dan took the phone out of its box. 'Hey, have you had a go on this already? It's switched on.'

'Sorry, I did have a look at it on the ride home. I just wanted to check that it was working ok. Hold on, I've got to show you this!' Katie snatched the phone out of Dan's hand.

'Hey, it's meant to be mine, don't forget!'

'I know, but I've got my spin class in half an hour and I wanted to show you a couple of things on it before I go.'

'Crack on, be my guest,' shrugged Dan.

'It's got this excellent predictive text amongst other things.'.

'Really? That's pretty much what's missing from my life right now.' Dan's lack of interest was palpable.

Katie typed away at a sentence.

'Let's try something challenging. What's that book you're reading at the moment, the Science Fiction one?'.

We'll Always Remember Paris.' Dan replied.

Katie perused the phone's personal organiser.

'OK, here we go....organiser....personal calendar....'

'...There's nothing new about a phone with a personal organiser and reminders, Katie'.

'Well it is to you, because you never made use of them....and you need to start using them! Anyway, where was I...ok, go to reminders...um … here.'

She passed the phone back to him.

'Start typing that title into your reminders for tomorrow. Just see how well it works'.

Dan began typing the short book title. Sure enough, every word was predicted from the first or second letter.

'Hmm ... that's cool,' said Dan. 'That was a fluke, surely?'

Katie shook her head. 'Always the pessimist! No fluke. We're right here in Toronto, and along with China, we're at the centre of 5G technology. The developed world is running on it. Data sharing, artificial intelligence, driverless cars ...'

'...Yet you still catch the tram. I just see disruption, not continuity,' huffed Dan.

Katie gave him a stern look, then continued.

'It shares and stores information and data as soon as it's first turned on. You're not the only person who's read that particular book. The software is so advanced now Dan, and this is the best on the market. Predictive text is pretty much one hundred per cent spot on. Try another title.'

'Will do. Let's see how this one goes. This book is turning out to be a prophecy as far as I can see!'

Dan began typing. The words quickly began to appear on the phone's small screen, *'Do...Androids...Dream...of...Electric....'*
Dan stared at the screen in amazement, until the final word appeared, *'...Sheets..'*.

'Are you sure you got the right model?', he chuckled.

'I'm just trying to help. So it's not one hundred per cent completely accurate yet. At least you managed to laugh for the first time in a while. Perhaps it needs time to get to know you!'

'Know me?' Dan spluttered. 'Don't start all that "Unseen Guardians" stuff. It'll only get me paranoid!'

'I don't want to hear that, Dan. You need to be in control of your .... problems now. I can't ... I mean we can't afford any set-backs.'

Dan let out a low groan at hearing this. Katie continued to lecture him in her usual headlong fashion.

'This is how the world works now, so get with it. It's about keeping you focussed, maintaining your health. Especially when you get back to work.' She took a breath.

'I told you about our logistics manager at work. Jesus, his watch saved his life! It was monitoring his heartbeat, then automatically sent a call out for an ambulance when he fell unconscious.'

'Did he survive?' Dan asked sardonically.

'Uh...no, he didn't. But that's besides the point. You've got your second session with Dr Adams tomorrow haven't you?'

Dan nodded.

'Well then, let's put a few reminders on there. Now, I know I'm meant to start the late shift, but I've switched with Rachael. So let's meet for some food after your appointment.'

'What time are you finishing work?'
'I'm aiming for 3, and your appointment is at
1:30. So that should work out fine.'

Dan made a couple of reminder notes set to go off at 11am the next morning,

'Dr Appointment 1pm.....Katie lift...Shift Days'. The predictive text was hundred per cent correct this time.

'Do you need to make a note of ... you know, taking your meds and stuff ... times and things?' Katie asked cautiously.

'Jesus, I'm not a ninety year old!'

'Of course. Well I'm going to get ready for my class. I'm meeting Rachael for a drink after that. I owe her a couple of drinks for swapping shifts with me tomorrow. Oh, that's another thing, you can get this great App on there called *Sleepscapes*. It plays music, sound effects and voice overs. They change every night. Amazing!'

'With these meds, I'll already be sound asleep by the time you get back.'

Dan put the phone back on the table.

Katie picked it up again.

'I'll just put something on there, for tomorrow on your way into town. You know, in case I need something.'

Katie showed him the reminder *Call Katie* on the screen, then put the phone back on the table.

'I have to go. Bye,' she said as she rushed out.

Dan left the apartment at mid-morning the next day. He hadn't ventured out very often over the past few weeks, but today he felt just a semblance of self-possession, just a little less fragile. He headed to his favourite coffee shop before getting the Transit Tram into the Quayside Sector. This 12 acre steel and glass spectacle along the waterfront had been proclaimed by the government as the 'Utopian Tech-Driven' area. It was where Katie worked, and also only a short walk from Dr Adams' clinic.

As Dan sat at his table sipping his flat white and skimming over the front page of the Metro Newspaper, his phone's alarm went off. Dan checked the phone. The reminder *'Dr Appointment 1pm ... Katie lift ... Shift Days,'* appeared on the screen.

'Yep, already out and on my way. I remembered that one,' he said to himself.

Twenty minutes later, Dan left the coffee shop and made his way to the tram stop, just 50 metres down the opposite side of the road. His phone alarm went off again. This time *Call Katie* appeared. He shook his head knowing that he would have completely forgotten to do that. He'd been asleep last night when Katie had finally arrived home. The Sleepscapes App had actually helped.

Dan arrived at Dr Adams' clinic fifty minutes later after a tram change at Carnival Square. Dr Adams' receptionist recognised him as he entered the foyer.

'Mr Mills. I do apologise, but Dr Adams couldn't make it in today. His wife has had an accident at home. He's had to cancel all his appointments for the day. We did try to contact you late yesterday afternoon and this morning, but we were unable to get through or leave a message. I am very sorry.'

'Uh ... that's ok. It must be this new phone. I didn't receive anything.' He checked the phone again. 'Nope. It's meant to be an all singing and dancing state-of-the-art thing, but that's obviously not a great start. I'm meeting my partner in an hour or so for lunch anyway. She works in the Walden Tower Block. It's not far from here.'

'That's an amazing building.'

'Yes, she's doing well. Better than me, that's for sure. She's the Assistant Advertising Manager for one of the Big Tech firms. It's all happened pretty quickly to be honest with you.'

'I'm pleased for you both. Well at least it wasn't a complete waste of time coming here then. I'll make you another appointment right away.'

Another appointment was agreed for the same time the following week. Dan headed out into the open air and towards the small park area in the heart of Quayside. He decided against buying cigarettes, but couldn't resist another coffee. A bench beside a pleasant boating lake provided him with a little sanctuary before meeting Katie.

As Dan gazed out over the small lake, his phone went off. Maybe that message from Dr Adams' clinic is finally coming through, he thought to himself. He put his coffee down and took his phone out of his satchel. *Call Katie* said the reminder. Dan nodded.

'Shit. Yes, of course.' He made the call. Straight to answer service.

'Hi. It's me obviously. My appointment was cancelled...uh believe it or not, this wonder phone didn't receive their message. Anyway, I'll meet you at that place across from your office...that Callum's Bar. I'll be there for 3pm. Let me know if there's a change ... I'll um ... hopefully get a message from you. Bye.'

Dan touched the screen to end the call. The reminder was still on the screen. It looked different though. The font had changed, it now appeared as *ɜXαλλ Κατιɜ*. He pushed his hair out of his eyes and took off his sunglasses before taking another look. This time it read *Kill Katie*. He dropped the phone on the floor and stared out onto the lake in shock. Panic started to set in. The sweating, the shaking, and the uncertainty began to take hold of his being. He stood up and paced up and down a few steps, whilst doing his best to control his breathing.

'What the fuck? ... what the fuck? ... What was that?' he whispered to himself over and over, before he worked up the courage to look at the phone's screen again.

Still shaking, Dan eventually picked the phone up. 'Jesus, did I just see that?' He flipped open the cover and swiped the screen which was now cracked in the centre. The reminder was still there, but now it read *Call Katie*. Again. He shoved the phone back in his shirt pocket and made his way to meet Katie.

Dan got to Callum's Bar within twenty minutes. He was still shaken up. The back of his shirt was covered in sweat, from both the heat and his anxiety. Katie was already there, stood by the bar talking to another woman. It was Rachael, her friend from work. Rachael spotted Dan first.

'Hey there! It's been a while. Woah, have you been jogging in those clothes or something?' she giggled.

'No, just walked across from the park. It's always humid around here. Good to see you by the way,' he said, struggling to make eye contact.

'You do look a little worn out,' Katie said, looking concerned. 'I'll get you a beer. Come on, our table's just here. Hey Rachael, enjoy your afternoon of retail therapy! I'll see you tomorrow.'

'Are you sure you're OK Dan? Maybe it was because your appointment with Dr Adams was cancelled.'

'Yeh, maybe.'

'Wow, you've nearly finished that beer, and we've literally just sat at our table!'

Dan took the phone out of his shirt pocket and put it on the table.

'It's ... um ... cracked. Sorry, I dropped it.'

'What? You've had it less than a day!'

'Look.' He showed Katie the reminder, 'The text ... the font I mean. It's changed by itself.'.

Katie examined the screen.

'Must be a glitch. It looks like the old 'symbol' font, like ancient writing. I've got that font on my phone and my PC. Just one of those things. Yes, a glitch, that's all. It just says *Call Katie*. Hi, I'm here!' she said, peering into Dan's face with a smile. 'So what, now don't tell me that's made you anxious again?'

'No, it looked ... it said something else. I'm sure it did ... ,' Dan muttered cautiously.

'How could it say something else? Well, what did it say?'

'I thought it said … it … it just wasn't what you put on there … it must be that font. A glitch like you said. I've slept so much these last few days. After weeks of near insomnia, it must be making me confused.'

'Too much sleep can't be a bad thing. Maybe you're coming off your medication too soon. You're still riddled with self-doubt … and please stop shaking! You know, that new emotional intelligence App is supposed to be great for …'

'… Please Katie, no more Apps for the time being!'

'It's your first time down-town for a while. Let's just have some food here, get a cab home, and then have some wine and watch a movie. I've got a late start tomorrow.'

Dan nodded in agreement, before finishing the rest of his drink.

'Yes, you're right. I'm riddled with self-doubt.'

After a near sleepless night, Dan waited for Katie to leave for work before getting in touch with Dr Adams' office. He made an appointment for the following day and went back to bed to try and get some sleep. He played around with the phone for a short while, before turning on the Sleepscape App. The narrator's calming voice and the tranquil sound effects worked as well as they had the previous night.

Around an hour later, Dan was awoken by his phone. It was another reminder. He got up, swilled his face with water and sat back on the bed. Then he checked his phone. The blinds were still drawn, so the light in the room wasn't good. There it was again, *Χαλλ Κατιε*. It was almost a sick kind of relief to see it there. The altered font. Just as Katie had said, it was just a glitch. It wasn't what he had seen, or thought he'd seen yesterday.

He opened the blinds and windows and got up to make himself a coffee. Then he sat on the sofa and picked up his phone. There they were again, the chilling words he had temporarily seen yesterday, *Kill Katie*. No font change, just there in plain letters. This time, Dan dropped the phone and his coffee. He didn't feel the hot liquid scald his thighs. His chest felt like it was going to explode, and his mind raced almost beyond control. He jumped up out of the chair and circled the room, terrified.

'Oh no … please no … this isn't happening … this can't be happening … ,' he spluttered to himself.

He rushed into the bathroom and jumped into the shower, still wearing his fatigues. The cold water cooled him down, but he was still in a state of terror. After a few terrible moments trying to compose himself, he picked his phone up off the floor. It nearly slid out of his wet, clammy hands. It was still there, that horrifying and surreal message, *Kill Katie.*

'What ... how is this happening? ... this isn't happening ... how can a phone do this ... it isn't me ... I ... I can't be this ill ...'

Dan threw the phone onto the sofa, quickly got dressed, and raced out of the apartment. He was headed towards the Communication Hub just outside the entrance to their apartment building. Barely controlling his shaking hands, he managed to tap in his personal four digit code. The sliding door of the small cylindrical unit opened and Dan typed his Comm-Card for instant Skype access. A pretty young woman's face appeared on the screen in front of Dan.

'Monument Advertising Agency, how may I help you today?'

'I..I..need to speak to Katie Sutton. Can you tell her it's … it's urgent …'

'It looks like Miss Sutton is available, I'll just try and put you through. One moment please.'

Dan wiped his face dry with the sleeve of his jacket as Katie's face appeared on the screen.

'Dan, is everything ok? Why are you using the Hub? What happened to your phone?'

'..Uh..I can't explain here, like this. Please, are you able to come home? I need to … to show you something …'

'Are you serious? Explain what? God, you look terrible. Ok, I'll try and get back in an hour or so.' She sighed before hanging up.

The screen went blank, and Dan headed back to the apartment.

Just over an hour later, Katie arrived home. She found Dan sat at the small kitchen table. He was staring into space. His phone was in the middle of the table.

'What the hell is going on Dan?'

Dan pointed to his phone.

'It did it again. The reminder. Just like yesterday. Check it, go on. Check my reminders.'

Katie dropped her shoulders and shook her head in disbelief.

'The phone....the fucking phone? That font thing that happened yesterday?' Her voice rose as she began to lose her temper.

'Are you seriously telling me that I came all the way back here for a stupid little glitch on your personal organiser? Jesus Christ Dan! Is it going to be the television next? What the hell is going on with you? Again!'

'Just take a look at the damn phone will you?' Dan yelled back at her.

Katie picked up the phone, flipped open the cover and stared at the screen. Dan noticed that her face bore no expression. She typed in Dan's password and looked through his personal organiser.

'There, now you look,' she said calmly, putting the phone in front of Dan on the kitchen table. 'You look Dan. There it is, from today, the same as yesterday, and every weekday for the next few weeks.'

Dan reluctantly looked through his organiser, shaking his head.

'What do you see Dan? Hopefully the same as me. The font has changed, like I said yesterday', she said, struggling to contain her anger.

'Fuck the font! It wasn't that, for Christ's sake!' Dan jumped out of his chair and threw the phone across the room. 'I know what I saw. It was something terrible ... unthinkable.'

Katie was silent for a moment. Then,

'You're clearly still not well. This relapse you're having, it's exacerbating all your problems.'

'Relapse? I wasn't that bad to begin with Katie! Get that thing away from me!' Dan cried as he crashed onto the sofa.

'Fine. I don't want to see you like this, I really don't.'

Katie walked over to where the phone lay on the floor and smashed it up with a few well-placed stamps from her heeled boots.

'There you go. It's gone. Have my phone. I'll get another this afternoon. We have to keep in touch. Especially with you in this state. You looked like a mad man when you called me from the Hub earlier. That's my workplace. I'm sorry to bring it up now, but my job is the only thing keeping a roof over our heads. You obviously won't be going back to work at the bookstore any time soon.'

'I see less and less of you Katie!' he cried.
'Please don't go there. Are you listening to me?
I can't be your carer!' she howled back at him.

Katie picked up what was left of Dan's phone and threw it in the trash bin.

'I can't leave you here alone like this. I'll have to stay home today, but I have to go in tomorrow ... I just have to. I'm meeting with someone really, really important.'

Dan looked at her through tear-stained eyes.

'I have an appointment tomorrow with Dr Adams. I'll explain everything to him. I'm obviously losing my mind.'

The spring heatwave had suddenly given way to stormy weather. Dan was awoken by the wind and the rain lashing against the bedroom window. He struggled more than ever to get out of bed. He'd been awake until the early hours of the morning, haunted by his experiences. Katie had got up and left earlier than usual. After yesterday, Dan was expecting that.

He took a shower, got dressed and began to prep himself for his appointment with Dr Adams. He started to shake again at the thought of explaining his madness to a psychiatrist. He shuddered with horror. Had his health actually deteriorated to the point that he believed that a smart phone could be sending him these insidious commands?

Just then, Katie's phone went off. She had left it at the apartment for Dan, as promised.

'It must be her ... maybe wishing me the best for today,' thought Dan. His spirits

lifted slightly, but paranoia still made him hesitate before checking the phone. Dan looked at the screen through half closed eyes. It was a severe weather warning for the next 24 hours. He let out a deep breath, put the phone in his coat pocket, and headed out.

The weather was becoming as severe as had been forecast. Dan wondered if the public transport would be running as usual. He had to make it to his appointment that morning. Realising that his umbrella wouldn't last a second in these gales, he pulled his coat over his head and made his way to the tram stop. As he did so, Katie's phone went off again. Dan had to check it, he was certain it would be Katie this time. It wasn't. The same sinister words he had seen over the past few days were there again.

'Kill Katie'

Now these words were on Katie's phone. Another phone, another device displaying this message. As Dan stared at the screen, frozen in terror, the words began popping up repeatedly. Over and over again, they appeared like a virus alert. Filling each hour and each day in the phone's calendar.

Dan switched from his state of frozen terror, to complete mania. He ran into the coffee shop and saw the barista Chang behind the counter.

'Hey Dan. Looks like you got caught in this terrible weather. The usual?' she asked.

Dan raced up to her and shoved the phone in her face.

'Please ... please, look at the screen and tell me what you see!'

'You don't look well Dan. Is ... is everything ok?'

'Just tell me what you see on the fucking screen!' Dan yelled back at her.

The young barista looked at the screen, then back at Dan in shock.

'It's just a reminder … it just says to call your fiancée,' she replied. Her voice was trembling.

'No … no … this isn't happening!' Dan cried.

By now everyone in the room was staring at him with a mixture of fear and concern.

'These aren't hallucinations … delusions … they can't be … someone else must be able to see this happening!' he screamed, before charging back outside.

He took one last look at the phone. The words *'Kill Katie'* were still popping up continuously as they had done before he went into the coffee shop. Now he was frantically and aimlessly running along the side-walk, crashing into anyone who got in his way. Soaked to the skin and breathless, he looked like an animal at the end of a cruel hunt. Still clutching Katie's phone, Dan raced into the road and was hit side-on by the very driver-less tram he had been meaning to catch. He was killed instantly.

The official verdict on Dan's death was suicide. Media reports were awash with stories of a disturbed man running and screaming through a busy suburb of Toronto, before jumping in front of a tram.

Less than a week later, Katie Sutton was calmly stepping out of an elevator on the top floor of the Walden Tower Block. Just opposite the elevator were two imposing oak doors. Katie stood still facing the wall to the left of the doors while a security screen scanned her eyes. The doors immediately opened, and Katie walked into a large open-plan office and living space.

A stocky man wearing an expensive suit was sat behind an over-sized black desk at the back of the room. The glass wall directly behind him offered a staggering night-time view of the city and beyond.

'You ok?' he asked Katie without looking up from his computer screen.

'Well I'm here, so I suppose so,' she answered. She slumped onto the Eames lounge chair in front of his desk.

Katie lit a cigarette and kicked off her shoes.

'Actually,' she said, letting out a puff of smoke, 'I think I may be … in a kind of state of shock.'

'Shock? I wasn't expecting to hear you say that. This has worked out better than we planned. He's dead, not jabbering on to some stupid shrink!'

'I guess I'm just shocked by a few things.'

'Namely?'

'Well, I suppose just how well your plan worked.'

'Our plan. You were just as eager to play this out as me, don't forget.'

'Sorry. You know what I meant. I thought it would take longer ... and maybe he would have twigged that something was going on other than losing his mind. Maybe someone else would've seen the things he was being sent.'

The man laughed and shook his head.

'We've long moved on from just basic crowd surveillance stuff now. This is what the future holds for us. The technological revolution is becoming part of our natural environment. Now a smart phone can recognise faces, key words and phrases. Just like some animals, or insects. Both your phones were fitted with facial recognition software. Although we had to take the chance that he'd only show you the phone, or what it said on the screen. If it wasn't your eyes or his eyes looking at the screen, and someone else looked at it, then that symbol font would appear. Another person would just realise that he was confused. Or worse. The phone was just a link to his fragile mind. We took a gamble, with this ... game.'

'I thought it would have been easier to just leave him after he'd lost his mind. I suppose I'm sounding naïve here, but I didn't expect him to take his own life like that.'

'This City needs to function in the best possible way. Especially if we are going to compete against London and New York for the world's wealthiest and most powerful citizens. This just proved to me how easily our residents' lives can be tracked, watched and altered if needed ... and rewarded or penalised, of course.' He got up from behind his desk.

'I need a drink. I'm sure you need one too.'

'Yes I do. Thanks.' She took a pull on her cigarette.

'As I told you when we first met, Katie, you deserve better.'

'Well, I wasn't going to spend the rest of my life caring for him, riding trams into work with the masses. I work hard, and I'm ambitious and gifted. It wasn't fair! He was unable to provide ... not even children!' She stared at him coquettishly. 'I wanted to be a part of your world. I wanted you.'

'And now you are part of my world. Exploitation is a primary function, the will to power, the will to succeed. He was weak, but you are strong.' He leaned over and kissed her.

'...and beautiful, I might add.'

THE END

STICKS AND STONES

Carl Fearnley and Warren Atkinson were sat in the bar of the Riverside Inn, on the banks of the Neesh river. It was an early June evening, and pleasantly warm. The place was quiet.

'Nice job they've done in here. It used to be an old boat-house. Eighteenth century according to the landlord,' said Warren as he sipped his pint of craft ale.

'It's alright. A bit too understated for me maybe. Not too expensive though,' Carl answered, fiddling with his well-worn cadet cap as was his habit.

Warren made a surreptitious roll of his eyes.

'Fair play mate, you've always had a critical eye on things.'

'Better than being like you though, innit? Mr Pollyanna. Everything's nice and cosy, everyone's a friend,' replied Carl.

'Knob,' Warren muttered under his breath.

Warren was used to Carl's hyper-critical nature. They'd known each other for nearly twenty years. Lately though, Carl had become increasingly intense and critical of people. Even with his friends and family, his vitriols were becoming unbearable. Warren just put it down to a midlife crisis. Failed relationships, missing out on that important promotion at work, and all that kind of stuff. Warren was a calmer, more contented individual. He could tolerate Carl's prickly personality, but of late, not many others could.

Two attractive women walked in with drinks in their hands and sat near the bar. They instantly caught Warren's eye.

'Clock that pair mate. Classy types they are. Looks like they're from down Bishop's Dale way. I'm glad I kept this blazer on now!' he said as he straightened himself up in his chair.

Carl shook his head with disdain.

'You look like such a tart in that garb, like you're auditioning for a holiday camp or something.' He glanced over to the women, and back to Warren.

'And you need glasses fella. The tall one looks like a pantomime horse.'

'Aw for fuck's sake, here we go again with your bloody standards' moaned Warren. 'What *are* you talking about? Nothing wrong with them, and there's nothing wrong with this blazer either. At least I've made an effort, unlike you, you ... scruffy bastard!' he spouted out in a rare show of temper. 'How did you become so mean and spiteful eh? You're going to end up a sad old man the way you've been behaving lately.'

Carl took no notice of Warren's censure of him. He just finished his pint and stood up.

'Whatever. I'm going out for a smoke. It's your round. Get them in. I'll have the same again.'

By the time Carl came back to the table, Warren had been to the bar and was now waving politely to another two women a couple of tables away.

'Well, I hope you're going for the old bag,' Carl said as he sat down.

'Don't now, mate. They live by me. Mother and daughter. The daughter's name is Winter. She's very quiet, but nice enough.'

'She's quite pretty I suppose. Looks a bit like that pantomime horse you were admiring just now … certainly got legs like one anyway. Winter … that's a funny name, innit? Are they amateur dramatic types then?' Carl asked.

Warren scratched his forehead nervously and stared down at the floor, ' … uh, no, they're Wiccans actually. They stick to themselves mostly. The father went missing a couple of years ago. A right bastard apparently.'

'Wiccans? … what the fuck? … is that like a Wookie or something? The mother's more a Jabba the Hutt type!' Carl began to babble on now. 'Talk about a pig's head. Have you seen the bingo wings on that old crow? Jesus…I think she might have eaten her husband, that's how he's gone missing!' He burst out laughing at this last quote.

'Fuckin 'ell, keep it down. They heard you then.' Warren was doing his best to hide behind his pint of cider.

'Wiccans, you know, white witches, ancient pagan rituals and all that. All harmless stuff I'm sure' he said quietly to Carl.

It was to no avail. Carl had downed his fourth pint of ale and was becoming more boisterous.

'Mumbo jumbo bollocks that is!' he spluttered. 'They need to get in the real world, people like that do. Weirdos. Probably bloody scroungers as well.'

Carl glanced over to them. The daughter stared back at him, whilst the mother quietly sipped her wine.

'Hey mate, I think the daughter might have heard me,' Carl said as he turned to Warren. 'She's just given me a right frosty look…get it? Frosty look?….Winter…frosty look?'

Warren sat still without acknowledging his friend. His face was flushed with embarrassment.

'Anyway, you're a boring twat. I'm going for a piss, and then I'll get the drinks in.' With that, Carl made his way to the toilet.

Warren built up the courage to turn to Winter and apologise, but she had gone. The mother sat alone gazing at the opposite wall. She appeared to be miles away. Warren just hoped that she had been oblivious to Carl's malicious comments.

When Carl came out of the gents' toilets, he saw Winter standing in front of him in the hallway. She stood still, staring right through him.

'You won't find your father in there love,' Carl sneered. 'The Ladies' are a bit further down there,' he added as he pointed further down the hall.

'I almost pitied you, but you don't deserve pity now.' She sighed as her light blue eyes suddenly turned dark violet. She stood rigid, glued to the spot, staring deeply into Carl's watery eyes, before grabbing hold of his arm.

'Hey, get your hands off me, you freaky bitch!' he cried.

'No, I won't find him in there. No one will find him,' Winter purred back at him.

A large moon-shaped pendant around her pale neck began to glow. Carl flinched with shock, but then he was suddenly powerless, unable to move away. Winter glanced behind her, then turned back and focussed her cold gaze on Carl.

In a low and menacing tone, she began to speak into Carl's ear.

'Sticks and stones may break my bones, but names can never hurt me … but they will hurt you, just as you use them to try and hurt others. They will haunt you and harm you … they will change and rearrange you.'

Then she let go of his arm, closed her eyes, and whispered to herself, 'I banish this one. This negative influence, I banish thee.'

Carl's body shook ever so slightly for a moment and his eyes closed. Winter then walked swiftly back to her mother at their table.

Carl opened his eyes and looked around him. He felt dazed and confused, and his head thumped with pain. He slowly made his way back to Warren in the bar. When he got there, Warren was talking to the two attractive women he'd been eyeing up earlier. Warren noticed Carl approaching.

'Where have you been mate? Thought you'd gone home and left me!' He turned to the women and introduced them to his friend.

'This is Chloe and Liza. They're on a training course in town for a few days.' He gave Carl a sly wink. 'Ladies, this is my old mate Carl. Hey…you alright Carl? You don't look too well. Don't worry about that Winter and her mother, they drifted out of here a few minutes ago.'

'Who?' Carl asked, genuinely confused.

'What do you mean, who?' replied Warren, an equally confused look on his face. 'The bloody mother and daughter you were just doing your best to offend,' he muttered under his breath.

'Yeah … yeah … mother and daughter … Listen, I'm not feeling too good. I … I must've had a … a … bad pint or something. I think I'll uh … make a move …'

'Are you sure mate? You don't seem yourself, mind you. I'll call you a taxi. You don't mind if I stay here do you?'

' … Uh … no, I don't mind. I think I'll walk though. My uh … my head is spinning. Fresh … uh … fresh air might help,' stuttered Carl.

'OK, as long as you're sure. Just take your time. You haven't got far to go anyway. I'll give you a bell in the morning, to see how you are. Take it easy.'

'Yeah … will do.' And with that farewell, Carl wandered out into the clear moonlit night and headed home.

On the short walk home, Carl meandered along mumbling and grumbling to himself, with his head still banging like a badly tuned bass drum. 'Bad pint … must've been a bad pint … poncy … pale … ale … ' He spat out the last few words.

Just as he arrived home, he could feel his legs and his back cramp up, as if he'd been poisoned. In his confused state, it almost felt to him that his legs were starting to shrink in length. And width.

He stumbled through his front door and up the stairs towards his room. His back continued to cramp up more and more on his way up the staircase, and he lost his footing once or twice. Once up the stairs, he headed straight for his room. He managed to get the key in the door. In doing so, Carl noticed that his hands appeared to look bigger and wider. The hair on the back of his hand was noticeably thicker, almost in the fashion of a down. His head was thumping louder now, booming in unison with his heartbeat. The noise was echoing around his head, a head which now seemed to fill the room. Before he knew it, Carl was crashed out on his bed. The blinds and window were still wide open, leaving the room awash with the sapphire hue of the brilliant moonlight.

Carl woke himself up early the next morning with a loud oink-like snore. It almost rattled the walls. He slowly opened his eyes and saw that his room was still covered in a strange blue hue. Carl went to put his hand to his face. When he did so, a large wing, like that of a gigantic crow, crashed into his beside cabinet. Carl jumped up out of what remained of his bed. It was now just planks of broken wood, with a mangle of sheets and mattress crumpled onto the floor.

What was left of Carl was also mangled. He caught sight of himself in the full length wall mirror. His appearance was a nightmare patchwork of different creatures, far worse than anything the warped minds of Dr Moreau or Dr Frankenstein could have concocted. He now possessed the legs of a horse, the torso of a man, the head of a boar, and of course, those two-foot-long crows' wings which had replaced his arms and hands. Carl let out a scream that came out as an almighty squeal.

'Carl, Carl, what the hell is going on!' Carl's housemate Jenny was banging on his door. 'You kept me and Stephen awake all night with all that loud crashing around. It sounds like you've got a bloody farmyard in there. Are you ok? Carl, Carl, … are you alright?'

Carl, or what was left of Carl, couldn't answer. Out of instinct, the creature that was Carl threw itself out of the bedroom window. With a flap or two of its wings, the monster glided to the end of the garden. It eventually made it to the fields and woodlands behind, but not before smashing through a neighbour's derelict greenhouse.

The disappearance of Carl Fearnley has never been solved. To this day, it remains a mystery that has shocked the residents of Neesh village. Not long after Carl's disappearance, chimerical stories began to circulate in the area. An abominable griffin-like beast prowling the woodlands at the edge of the village at night was reported by terrified children and young lovers. Well, by those who survived to tell the tale …

THE END

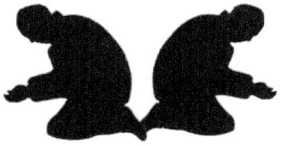

THE BEGGAR

A white Mercedes saloon pulled alongside the kerbside at the far end of St. Joseph's Road in the dying light of a mild early December afternoon. Inside the vehicle sat an attractive and smartly-dressed couple in their mid-thirties.

Ian loosened his tie and lowered the volume of the car stereo. He didn't feel comfortable in this neighbourhood. It was once a lively working class community, but over the past couple of decades it had really deteriorated. It was now one of the most notorious areas in the city. At any cost, Ian did not want to be there.

'Christ Danni, look at the state of this place. Did we have to make this call so late?'

'I'm sorry Ian, but yes we did. Mrs Dunn called into the shop at the last minute this afternoon. I'd already sent the girls home and it's a big order. She wanted the samples tonight,' said Danni.

'Yes I know it's business, but you knew we had the presentation tonight,' snapped Ian.

'Well I'm sorry, but I can't afford to pick and choose who buys my stock. And I can't afford to pass up an order like this. Bridal wear is very competitive these days, you know that much. The business has only been going for just over a year. Mrs Dunn doesn't have internet access or a mobile phone. She's a quirky old lady to say the least!'

Ian smoothed back his jet black hair and admired his own dark Celtic good looks in the rear view mirror. He was a handsome man, but his good looks were affected by a constant look of smugness.

'She must be bloody senile living in this dump, when she can afford to spend thousands on dresses for her daughter's wedding,' he barked.

Relenting, he sighed.

'Well, hurry up then darling. The Parkland Manor is a good twenty minutes from here, and I don't want to turn up when Brian Goodman is giving his speech. Where does this old biddy live exactly? Above that off-license?' He pointed to a corner shop that was partly covered in shuttering.

'Yes Ian,' said Danni impatiently. 'That's the entrance, those double doors next to the off-licence. There's a bell, then they answer and it's just up some stairs. I'll only be a few minutes.'

Danni grabbed the book of samples from the back seat, before turning to her husband with a smile. He smiled back at her.

'What about your coat Danni? It's starting to get cold out there.'

'I won't need it. I'll only be a minute.'

'In that case I'll keep the engine running.'

Danni gave him a quick kiss before leaving the Mercedes and making her way up to Mrs Dunn's flat.

Ian watched like a hawk as his pretty, petite wife headed for the flat. She looked very attractive in her black high heels and chic cream evening dress, her dark bobbed hair rising and falling with each stride. Such an appearance of elegance contrasted greatly with the semi-barricaded shop-front adorned with spray-painted obscenities. Danni rang the doorbell, waited a minute and then disappeared up the stairs that led to the flat.

Inside the Mercedes, Ian sat nervously in his charcoal designer suit. A swift scan of the dilapidated neighbourhood made his face grimace with disgust. Adjoining the off-license was a row of five squalid-looking Edwardian town houses. Next to the houses was an old church hall and a primary school. Both buildings were now derelict and imprisoned by the same eight-foot-high corroded iron railings. The opposite side of the road was busier, but also very scruffy. It boasted a mini supermarket, a community café, a kebab house and a laundrette.

Ian eventually spotted a man sitting on the pavement outside the community café about twenty feet away. The café was now closed for the evening, but the signage lighting was left on and it acted as a faint spotlight for the homeless man crouched below.

A chill was starting to set in and the man was wearing an old khaki-coloured parka jacket and a black woollen skull cap. He was covering himself from the waist down with a red blanket. Ian soon spotted that the man was holding a small container of some sort between his hands.

'Dear me,' Ian muttered to himself. 'Beggars this far out of town. What a bloody mess.'

As he took another sly glance at the sad figure that was sat hunched on the pavement, he suddenly realised that the beggar's face seemed familiar to him. Yes, he knew the man. He began to wonder when and how, trying to place him in a former time or situation without glancing back at him. The temptation was too much for his curious nature and as he took yet another surreptitious look, he noticed the beggar was staring back at him and the car. Within that brief second both men recognised each other. Ian jolted slightly and went back to fiddling with the car stereo.

Danni got back into the car.

'All done,' she said. She threw the samples on the back seat. 'She didn't even bother to look at the book, she knew what she wanted. I'm so pleased - this is great news.' She was beaming with delight. 'Right, let's go to this party!'

Ian put the car into gear and started to drive off.

Just then, two young men approached the homeless man. Both men were tall and wiry. One of the men was wearing a grey tracksuit, the other a dark hooded top and very loose jeans. They were obviously intoxicated as they swaggered menacingly towards the beggar. They stood over him laughing, then they began shouting and screaming at him.

'Oh God, hold on Ian! Look at that poor man!'

Ian had already noticed, but wasn't going to say anything.

'I hope they leave him alone,' said Danni.

But they didn't. The man in the tracksuit suddenly threw a can of beer at the beggar's head. Then both the men began kicking and stamping on him. As he rained blows onto his victim, the larger of the two fell over. They stopped their attack, but continued with more verbal abuse.

'Can't we do something? Phone the police, or get help?' Danni pleaded.

'No Danni. I'm not getting involved in any way, especially not tonight. Look at the state on them, this is probably a bit of fun for these people. I bet it happens all the time. He can beg for his shitty life for all I care.'

Ian checked his mirrors, swung the Mercedes around and drove off in the opposite direction.

'Sometimes I don't get you, Ian,' Danni cried as she slammed the car door shut. 'We could at least have phoned the police.'

'Just leave it there, will you girl? I've got a lot on my mind tonight. Don't start giving me shit over nothing!'

Ian surveyed the graceful surroundings of the Parkland Manor as they arrived for his work's Christmas party. His angry tone subsided as he spotted the other guests and dignitaries making their way towards the Georgian mansion house in their formal evening wear.

'Look, as I said earlier, that kind of thing probably happens every night. We don't owe anyone any favours. The guy's probably fine.' Ian took a deep breath and walked towards his wife. 'Come on. Let's not go in there all angry with each other.' He embraced her. 'We deserve a nice night out. And besides, I drew the short straw tonight. You can drink all the free wine and champagne that you like, I'm driving us home for a change.'

As Ian and Danni entered the main room of the manor house, they spotted Matt and Amanda, already seated at the company's table. The couple stood out among the crowd of people sat around the table. Matt was a stout, thickset man, as wide as he was tall. He had a round, jovial face and a mop of wavy, heavily-gelled red hair. Amanda was his meretricious trophy wife. A tall, slender blonde, she seemed to have a permanent look of mischief on her face. Matt beckoned them over. Both men worked as area sales consultants for C&C Private Medical Care for the past five years.

'Evening Mandy, evening Matt,' said Ian with his usual air of haughtiness, as he and Danni approached the table.

'Hey, you're finally here!' bellowed an already tipsy Matt.

'Yeh, bloody finally. Danni had to drop some samples off to this old woman in St Joseph's,' Ian replied with clear irritation.

'That's a dodgy area mate. You must have really stood out in that nice motor of yours.'

'I'm glad you made it here in one piece. You both look lovely, by the way,' Amanda chipped in.

'Is that the Hugo Boss suit you told me about, mate?' asked Matt.

'Yes. Nice, isn't it?' replied Ian.
'It shows off that athletic physique of yours,'
added Amanda coquettishly.

Danni broke into the conversation.

'That's all bloody gym work. He rarely goes outdoors, and he won't even take our daughter to the baths. That new personal trainer of yours, what's her name again Ian?'

Ian shot Danni a disapproving look while
Matt spoke up, attempting to cut short an impending quarrel.

'Hey Ian, before you get comfortable, come and have a chat with David Phelps. He's worried about his speech on the McAndrew deal. You know he was really keen to get a last minute opinion from you.'

The two men stood up and headed towards the bar while Amanda turned to Danni.

'Another little tiff on the way here?' she smirked.

'Not really Amanda. We saw an incident which upset me. Ian didn't seem too bothered though.'

'Oh please tell! What happened?' begged Amanda, her penchant for gossip evident.

'There was this awful fight outside that community café. Well not so much a fight, it looked like two guys were beating on this poor homeless guy.'

'Oh, that's terrible. You poor thing,' Amanda said insincerely.

'Well I'm more concerned about that man to be honest with you.'

'Oh, of course. It's awful Danni, but I know that place well. There's a lot of problems happening around that area, especially on that main road. Yes, a lot of terrible people hanging around involved in this and that. You know that café is trying to help these people, but there's still trouble. I just think that they're beyond help. Honestly, what can you do?' Amanda's lack of concern on the matter was tangible.

'Well perhaps I'm more sensitive to things like that,' replied Danni. 'I'm just not used to seeing it. I think we should have called the police. I just hope that he's ok. I know you and Ian grew up in a livelier part of town so to speak. I suppose you do toughen up to violence then.'

Amanda picked up the bottle of white wine next to her and proceeded to fill both her and Danni's glasses.

'Come on, give yourself a break for the evening,' Amanda said with a wink.

'Yes I really need that, but I have to use the loo first. I'll be back in two ticks.'

'Oh well, don't be long, I don't want to down this bottle in one go by myself,' chuckled Amanda as she swigged back most of her glass.

Ian returned to the table alone, sat down and poured himself a small glass of wine.

'Designated driver tonight then are we?' asked Amanda.

'Yes, I'm just having the one glass' Ian said. 'I don't mind though, Danni deserves a break.'

'She seemed upset about that fight between those homeless guys on St. Joseph's main road. Was it that bad then?'

'Well it wasn't pleasant, but I mean … you could phone the police and they might not even turn up.' Ian shrugged. 'C'mon Mandy, you know what Danni's like, old goody two shoes. Her and Matt have benefited from a nice middle class upbringing. They're not street-wise like us.'

Ian gazed admiringly at Amanda for a few seconds before staring down at the glass in his hand. Amanda momentarily placed her hand on top of his, before returning it to her own wine glass.

'Well for someone who claims they're not bothered about that trouble earlier tonight, something seems to be playing on your mind. What's wrong?' she asked.

'I recognised that homeless bloke, Mandy. He seemed to recognise me too. You remember the Beynon brothers from school don't you?'

'Yes, they were a right pair of loose cannons.' 'Yeah, they were. Well, I'm sure it was that Mikey Beynon. He was in a hell of a state mind you.'

'They had a rough time of it growing up though, Ian,' Amanda said, with a rare show of compassion. 'My friend dated his brother Rob for a while. He was around our age. I think Michael was three years younger than him. Come to think of it, they lived in the St. Joseph's area. I know Rob was always getting banged up. The last I heard of Mikey would have been … maybe … ten years back. He'd joined the Army. I think he was a paramedic or something.'

'Well it looks like he's back in town now, and clearly not a paramedic anymore. Yeah, Rob and Mikey.' Ian shook his head dismissively. 'Nuisances. Always up to no good, the both of them.'

Just then he spotted Danni making her way back to the table.

'Anyway, let's not ruin a good night on the likes of them. And there's no need to tell Danni about our conversation.'

Boutique Bridal was the first building in a row of pastel-coloured shops that lined Eden Way. A number of shops, including Danni's, had ornate continental-style canopies hanging above large well-decorated shop windows. It was a pleasant and busy suburb a mile outside the centre of town, popular with affluent shoppers. The opposite side of the road was filled with attractive wine bars, coffee shops and restaurants.

Danni was sat behind the counter busy checking her new stock arrivals on her laptop when a plump, smartly dressed woman of around seventy came into the shop.

'Mrs Dunn, how nice to see you. I put your order through the day after we spoke last week. Everything is going fine.'

'I just wanted to call in myself and thank you for calling over to my flat last week,' said Mrs Dunn. 'I do apologise for dragging you over to that part of town. We get problems there all the time.'

'Oh don't be silly, it's the least I could do,' said Danni. 'There was trouble outside that community café as we were leaving. Some poor homeless man was being attacked. I wanted to call the police, but my fiancé said he was probably intoxicated and it was pointless getting involved.'

'Yes, I heard about that. He was lying there unconscious for a while before Mr

Llewellyn the community café manager found him. Luckily he had only gone back to the premises by chance and found the poor man all bloody and bruised. Just think what might have happened.'

'Oh no, that's terrible news Mrs Dunn. I feel awful now.'

'My neighbour, Mrs Thomas, spoke to the manager of the café the next morning. Apparently that beggar had been taunted by some youngsters for a while. They were off their bloody heads probably. People seem to think that it's a laugh to abuse the homeless. I mean, they're people like you and me deep down. Who knows what their lives have been like? Well, they went too far that night. They've put him in hospital now.'

Both women stood silently for a moment before Danni said, 'I hope someone is able to help him.'

'I hope so too my dear,' replied Mrs Dunn. 'When you think of those poor souls, in the winter, all alone living out rough on the streets. Oh it gives me the chills just thinking about it.'

When Ian arrived home later that night, Danni's Audi A1 was already parked in the drive of their waterfront town house. Entering the front door that opened into a large open-plan living space, he saw Danni sitting alone at the dining table. She had undressed and put on her bathrobe and pyjamas. Her laptop was in front of her, but she was staring into space. Her elbows were perched on the table as she held a glass of wine with both hands close to her lips.
Ian took off his suit jacket and undid his tie before grabbing a wine glass out of the cupboard.

'Is Lucy still at your mum's then?' he asked as he poured himself a glass of wine.

'Mum and Katie have taken her and Jack to the Winter Wonderland Fair. She's staying at my parents' tonight. I was planning to go over some work this evening.'

'Oh right. I might as well have a drink then,' he said. 'It's been a bitch of a day at work,' he moaned. 'I think I'll order a takeaway. Have you eaten?'

'No, I'm not really hungry.'

Ian found some menus next to the fridge and made his way to the suede sofa which looked out onto their terraced balcony. Beyond that was a stunning stretch of coastline which was beautifully lit up by the reflection of a low full moon.

'Anything good on the box tonight then?'

'I don't know Ian. I'm busy and I'm not really in the mood for the television tonight.'

'You had a bad day or something?'

Danni sat back in her chair.

'Well yes, to be honest with you. Mrs Dunn, the old lady from St Joseph's Road, came in this morning.'

'She cancelled her order or something?' he asked as he perused his menus.

'No, the order's fine. But she mentioned the trouble there that night. That homeless man was really beaten up, those kids left him for dead. Apparently the manager of that community café found him by chance and called an ambulance."

'Really?' said Ian without looking away from the takeaway menu. 'You sure you don't want any
food?' He made no attempt to hide his lack of concern.

'No, I don't. It's been playing on my mind all day. What if that man hadn't found him Ian? We didn't do anything. He might have died.'

Ian dropped the menu onto the sofa and glanced over to her.

'Now don't look into this too much, will you Danni? How were we to know it was that serious? I haven't given him a second thought.'

Danni gazed out of the kitchen window and onto the quiet coastline in front of the house.

'I've always believed in Karma. You've got to give people a chance.' Her speech was more controlled now. 'What about our social responsibility?' she asked.

'What about being of some use to society?' Ian snarled with contempt. 'I've been lonely and miserable in the past. You can't go around being the martyr all the time. Honestly Danni, you've got to toughen up.'

Ian looked around their stylish home, filled with state-of-the-art electronics and designer furnishing. An ebony baby grand piano stood in the corner of the lounge. Danni had recently begun teaching Lucy on it.

'I've worked hard to get away from the rabble I grew up with. Look at this place. It's stunning,' Ian said with pride. 'I mean, we're barely into our mid-thirties. All this, and a beautiful daughter,' he added.

He walked over to Danni and placed his hands softly on her shoulders. He bit his lip for a couple of seconds before making his confession.

'Look Danni, I knew that bloke. From before, from when we were kids. Him and his brother, they were in school with me and Amanda.'

Danni turned in her seat and glanced up at him.

'What, so is it personal then?'

'What do you mean, is what personal?'

'Not helping that poor bloody man!'

'Well no, no, I just never liked them. They were a pair of cocky troublemakers. Honestly Danni, why do you care so much?'

'Jesus Ian, that was years ago! You're acting like a bloody child,' cried Danni. 'The man could have died and we did nothing. My brother Chris could have easily ended up the same way when he got into those financial problems!'

'Yes, and a bloody drug problem!' snapped Ian.

'Oh God, listen to you. Ian Collins, the bloody martyr! Look, the point I'm trying to make Ian, is that he had a family to help him out. We were all there for him!'

'Yes, but that's family though. It's different then. And anyway, my family didn't help me much. You know that my parents were a pair of piss-heads. I had to get on with it, put myself through college, got myself into debt … '

'Oh leave the working class platitudes aside for one night,' Danni interrupted. 'That's not quite the same, is it? You did ok. My father lent you money after we moved into our first flat.'

'It was just a couple of grand. I paid it off within a year!'

'Well, I just can't help but wonder what went wrong for this man.'

Ian grabbed the bottle of wine off the table and made his way back to the sofa, sitting himself down heavily. He poured a glass, then let out a deep breath and continued with his sanctimonious speech.

'We're not the bloody Samaritans. Some people are meant to get on in life and others aren't. It's all about survival. You'd never see me in that way, that desperate. Just the thought of it, begging for anything. Scrounging bastards. That's what I think of Karma' he sneered.

Steve Llewellyn sat behind the desk in his office at the back of the St Joseph's Road community café. The café served as a charitable organisation that aimed to promote awareness of homeless and vulnerable people in deprived areas such as St Joseph's.

Steve was a former sociology lecturer and ex-alcoholic who had set up the café after his retirement from teaching just over two years ago. He was a short, stocky man with long, shaggy, platinum-coloured hair. The pair of silver-rimmed granny glasses that sat on his bulbous nose added a few years to his wrinkled and ruddy face. Now a trained counsellor, he held monthly one-to-one mentoring sessions with many of the vulnerable people who visited the community café. Today as on most days, he was dressed casually in jeans and a red checked lumberjack-style shirt.

On the other side of Steve's desk sat a man in his early thirties, of slight build and gaunt appearance. He had close-cropped brown hair and a scruffy beard that gave an unnatural ruggedness to an otherwise boyish face. The man's left arm was in a plaster cast and the left side of his face was badly bruised. He wore an old navy-blue fleece cardigan and black, well-worn combat trousers. In his lap he held an old parka jacket and a rucksack.

'Well Mike, it's been a month since you were attacked. How are you feeling now?'

'I've been worse. It's the left side of my body where the pain is the most. I've got a broken hand and my cheek bone was fractured. Good job I'm right handed, innit!' Mike let out a childish giggle, then suddenly stopped before continuing in a more solemn tone.

'I'm still really shaken up to be honest with you. mate. It's been a few weeks, and I can handle myself, but I feel more vulnerable than ever before. There's so much hostility out there these days.'

Steve rested his elbows on his desk, took off his glasses and clasped his hands in front of his face, as if he were about to say grace. His reverential demeanour brought a sense of calmness and gravitas to these meetings.

'I'm so sorry Mike. Call me naive, but I didn't expect such trouble to happen here, just in front of the café. There again, you'll always have morons roaming the streets up to no good. I'm going to have security cameras outside from now on. It's a good job that you're a tough cookie.'

Mike shrugged his shoulders and stared at the floor.

'I'm really sorry as well mate. You've never had trouble here before and now there's this. I ... I just ... ,' Mike's voice began to break.

He took a deep breath before continuing.

'It doesn't matter what I do, I can't seem to get away from trouble. But let's be honest, I shouldn't have been outside the café in the first place.'

Steve pulled his chair forward and sat up in his seat, hands on his lap. His sympathetic nature would
often give way to sternness at the appropriate time. 'I was getting to that point. Look, we'll do everything we can to help you, you know that. But you've got to help yourself as well. Have you taken any of those legal highs lately?'

Mike looked at the floor and slowly shook his head.

'None of that bloody Spice stuff?' asked Steve.

Mike shook his head again, only more determinedly this time. He raised his head and looked Steve firmly in the eyes.

'No Steve, honestly. Just booze and pills. Tranquillisers mainly … if I can get my hands on them.'

Steve's tired features began to soften.

'Ok Mike. Next month we're going to begin weekly counselling sessions here. I've already spoken to the Sanctuary Foundation and the local authority this morning. I'm also confident we can find you accommodation. That's a very positive move for you,' Steve said with his indomitable enthusiasm.

Mike nodded silently in agreement. He trusted and liked the older man.

Steve rose from his chair and made his way to the other side of the room to make a pot of tea. He looked back to see Mike thumbing through some of the pamphlets on his desk.

'There are other charities that can help you as well, you know. You have to remember you're not alone. But for now, I think the most important thing for us to do is try and get you into accommodation. Then you can hopefully clean yourself up and perhaps begin some form of training. It could lead to employment and then …'

Mike interrupted Steve's oration.

'Look, you're a good bloke Steve, and I know you've had your own troubles, but you can't imagine what it's like when you've had a home, a family and a job only to lose it all.' Mike dropped his head into his hands. 'I was on the sail bridge the other day and these two women passed me. They were drunk and I was bloody sober. They'd probably been to one of those swanky bars over that way.' His voice was muffled as he began to sob.

'As they were coming closer to me, I could hear one of them saying, *God, he must be freezing. How can he live like that? I'd have topped myself if I was him!*'.

He began to straighten up and compose himself.

Steve placed a sympathetic hand on Mike's shoulder. 'Here, drink this mug of tea and give yourself a minute.'

Cup and saucer in hand, Steve went back to his chair and took a long sip of his own tea.

'A lot of people have been in a similar situation to you. Believe it or not they've come out of it.'

'It's not a life I've chosen,' said Mike.

'Most of what we do isn't about choice, Mike. A lot of people don't have a choice. You know as well as I do that these are harsh and divisive times we're living in. There are families out there, working families, who are destitute.'

He considered Mike's situation. He'd had a difficult life since childhood. His father was a fireman in the Army, offered a position in Germany, something that caused conflict between him and Mike's mother. He eventually accepted it and the couple divorced. He had rarely spoken to his father since. Mike's mother had battled with alcoholism. As a result, she struggled to raise Mike and his brother Rob by herself. Both brothers turned to drink and drugs as an escape from poverty and misery during their teens. This in turn led to petty crime, until in a moment of clarity, Mike himself joined the Army in his early twenties.

Both men sat quietly for a few minutes cradling their warm drinks. It was approaching winter and the temperatures outside were quickly dropping. The mid-December chill was already beginning to pervade the poorly heated room.

Steve broke the silence.

'You trained as a paramedic when you were in the Army, didn't you?'

'Yes. When I first joined up I wanted to train as a fireman like my dad, but I was getting panic attacks during the initial training. So I started the paramedic training. It didn't last long, about six months. I just wasn't disciplined enough.'

'Was that when the depression kicked in?'

'Well, it was probably before that. Before I joined, my brother was locked up in prison for a year. That finished my mother off. She died a few months later.' He paused, before steadying himself to continue. 'That's why I joined up I suppose. No one left. But yeah, I did go downhill about a year after I joined the Army. I was discharged on medical grounds.' His voice began to break again. 'I … I've struggled to hold down work or any kind of relationship ever since.'

'I'm sorry to bring that up Mike, I didn't mean to upset you. You've been through enough. But you have to remember that you're a good, capable man. You had that initial training. You have the skills that can help people, help save lives!'

Steve looked out of his office window. It was only three thirty, but another harsh winter night was already closing in.

'Where are you staying tonight?' he asked.

'I've got a couple of nights' shelter over in Bethesda House,' Mike said.

'Well at least you'll have some food and shelter then.'

'I still sleep around the coast as well, Steve. I got hold of a tent. People don't tend to take much notice in the summer and stuff, but it's hard work this time of year. It just makes me feel alive, you know? The air, and being left alone by the sea, away from the streets and the grime, and … ' he hesitated, thinking of how to describe himself, '....and other people like me.'

'Of course Mike. I understand.' Steve gave him a reassuring smile and a nod of the head. 'Ok then, let's leave it there for today my friend. I'm sure you'll be wanting to get to the shelter and settle in before tonight.'

Both men stood up and shook hands. As Mike was about to leave the room he turned to Steve and asked him a question.

'That night I was attacked, when you found me. I'd been laying there for a couple of hours hadn't I?'

'Yes, it was fortunate that I was coming to the café to collect my phone. I'd left it here earlier in the day.'

'So no one had actually called the police or anything?' Mike enquired.

'No, nobody did. Maybe people thought you were sleeping.'

'Yeah. But all the blood, it was all over the pavement … '

'Well I'm sure if there had been witnesses they would have helped,' Steve said reassuringly.

'There were witnesses though. There was this couple in a fancy car, a Merc. I recognised the guy from school.'

'Oh. Are you sure Mike? I mean, you had been drinking, and you've been through a lot of trauma since then,' Steve said in earnest.

Mike shook his head, 'No, no … it was definitely him. Ian Collins his name is. His number plate was I4N … something, something. I can't remember the rest. I4N … for Ian I should imagine. Always loved himself he did. Looks like he's done really well for himself now. He had a smart brunette with him. Probably his missus, although I've seen him before with some other tart, a tall blonde. They were walking around the coast, him and that blonde. They looked more than friends to me. I'm sure I remembered her from school as well. Yeah anyway, him and my brother were seeing this bird at the same time years ago, when we were kids. I think they had a fight over it. He got my brother beaten up afterwards. A bad loser, and a bad minded bastard!'

'And they definitely saw you being attacked? I mean that man and his partner in the car?' Steve asked cautiously.

'They must have. They were there when it started. I can't help but think - why didn't they do something?'

'I don't know Mike, maybe they had their reasons. Fear perhaps? Although I would hope that it wasn't out of malice. Try not to let this play on your mind. Give yourself some time to rest now. Go to Bethesda House for some food and warmth. No detours on your way back to the shelter, ok? And please, try and stay safe, warm, and out of trouble over Christmas my friend. Don't forget that we're here

Christmas Day if you can't make it to the Salvation Army.'

Mike put on his jacket carefully and picked up his bag.

'Yeah ok, thanks again mate. I'll probably see you then. I really appreciate everything you're doing for me.'

Both men shook hands again before Mike quietly left the café.

A year had passed, and with it another Christmas. As promised by weather forecasters, this time it had brought with it a paltry dusting of snow. It had officially been a white Christmas none the less. The cold and frosty conditions of that December were followed by an even colder January. The unforgiving winds from the east had accompanied the New Year celebrations, and continued well into the month.

On the afternoon of the last Saturday in January, Ian had taken Lucy to Rotherbrook

Bay. It was only a twenty minute drive from their home in the marina. Lucy had brought with her a kite that she'd had for Christmas. She spent the short journey studying the toy. It was brightly coloured in pink and lilac swirls, coating the kite's body. The colours almost matched the pink duffel coat and wellies that Lucy was wearing. The novelty of the surprise Christmas present from Danni's brother clearly hadn't worn off yet. Although it was quite a humble gift, Lucy loved it. Everyone had agreed that it was a great idea. Getting children away from a screen and out into the open was no mean feat these days.

Ian's Mercedes pulled into one of the parking bays that overlooked Rotherbrook bay. The bay stretched for nearly a mile. It had a sandy beach that was as breathtaking in the coldest of winter days as it was in the summer. As long as it didn't rain. Lucy hastily got out of the car.

'Hold on Lucy,' yelled Ian. 'I don't want you running off with that bloody thing. Wait for Daddy, and we'll walk down to the beach together. Lucy, I said … !' It was to no avail. Lucy had already bounded her way down to the sands clutching hold of the kite. Ian checked his hair and put on his Ray Bans before getting out of the car. After a couple of minutes, Ian caught up with Lucy on the shoreline.

'Look Lucy, I know you're excited, but stop running off will you? You've never flown one of these things before. It's more difficult than it looks, and I don't want any hysterics if you lose it straight away. Alright?'

Lucy nodded her head in acknowledgment.

'Will it work down here Daddy? I mean, it's not that windy is it?'

'Well, let's give it a go. I can show you how to hold it properly, and then we can take it further up around the coastal path. It's nice and quiet down here today, hardly anybody around.'

The next hour passed safely enough. Ian got to spend some much-needed and missed quality time with his daughter, while Lucy got to try her new kite out across the bay's coastline.

'Let's make our way down to the Brasserie, Luce. You've had a good time with your new toy. I wouldn't mind a swift drink and a bit of food after all this fresh air.'

As they made their way towards the Rotherbrook Brasserie, they reached a notorious section of the coastal path that formed a sudden and steep incline, followed by a sharp and crooked left bend. After this, the pathway dropped back down into a steep descent, and eventually back to sea level.

'Right Lucy, hold on to Daddy's hand, and give me the kite as well. It can get a bit dangerous on this climb. Be careful.'

Lucy held onto to Ian's hand, but refused to relinquish her beloved kite, which she held close to her chest.

'I want to hold the kite. It's mine,' she said.

Ian shook his head at Lucy, but gave in to her demands. He usually did. Everyone said that she was the spitting image of her father. She had certainly inherited his striking black hair, emerald eyes and high cheek bones.

'You're bloody spoilt and stubborn. Just like your mother! Just keep hold of it then, this wind is really starting to pick up.'

The sound of a dog barking some way behind them suddenly caught their attention. Ian looked back and saw that around fifty metres away, an elderly woman was doing her very best to jog along the path, while a buoyant fox terrier jumped up and down alongside her. It was obvious that the dog was wearing her out. Slowly but surely they were making their way towards the incline.

'Come on then Lucy, let's get a move on. I'm cold and hungry, it's getting dark and I'm getting blown about,' he whinged. 'And you just keep calm. I know you're as nervous of dogs as much as I am of that bloody water down there. It's only a little terrier, and it looks like it's on a lead. We'll let them pass now while we're at the bottom of this incline and then carry on as quick as we can. Ok?'

Lucy nodded, gripped Ian's hand tightly and held onto the kite. As they made their way, they heard the woman frantically shouting. The terrier had pulled free of its lead and was making its way towards them. Within a matter of seconds it had reached them, and was making a beeline for Lucy and her kite. Ian tried to scare the animal away with a kick of his leg, but it was to no avail. Ian soon turned his attention to the elderly woman, who had just caught up.

'Get this stupid dog away from me and my daughter, you stupid old cow!' he shouted.

Although the little terrier was just over-excited and eager to play, Lucy's fear of dogs got the better of her. She threw her hands up in the air, which meant letting go of her new prized possession. In confusion, Lucy then grabbed for the kite again with one arm, whilst shielding herself from the dog with the other.

Within a split second, Lucy fell backwards between a small gap in the rickety wooden railings that ran between the path and straight into the cold water below. It was at the beginning of the incline, where the drop was only around seven feet. Fortunately, it was high tide, so it was a sheer drop straight into the water. If she'd fallen in further up the path, Lucy would have landed on one of the large rocks jutting out of water. It was also fortunate that the current was mild, but it was still strong enough to drag her away from the land. Her kite, now forgotten, was drifting off into the darkening sea behind her.

She could barely swim, but the bright young child's survival instincts kicked in. She could try and make her way to the ragged coastal wall, or to the nearest rock. The rock was closer to her than the thin edge of land. Either way she would have to hold on for dear life. Fighting her overwhelming panic, Lucy kicked her legs as hard and fast as she could to make the rock.

Ian was frozen in shock. It all happened so quickly, he was unable to take in that his daughter was fighting for her life.

Then he suddenly realised that Lucy was trying to make her way to safety.

'Lucy! Lucy!' he screamed. 'Just keep going. Kick your legs and try and get to that rock!'

'I'm so sorry, this is my fault,' sobbed the woman beside him. 'He just came off the lead.' She was clearly upset.

'You stupid, stupid cow!' Ian shouted at her.

'You must jump in and save the poor child!' she cried back at him.

Ian stood at the edge of the bank, his attention fixed on his daughter's struggle to get out of the water. His initial anger with the woman soon turned into a desperate plea for help.

'Please help me. It must be freezing ... what am I going to do? I can't swim ... I can't swim!' he screamed in despair.

'But ... you have to go in ... you'll have to. For God's sake man!" she replied, exasperated by Ian's admission.

Ian grabbed the woman by the arm.

'You can go in there, I'll hold onto you!'

I'm not strong enough to save her!' she insisted. 'Call 999 now!'

'I ... I left my phone in the car. There's no signal here. I didn't think I'd need it,' Ian blurted out.

The woman looked at Ian in disbelief, and then looked out to Lucy who was now clearly struggling to get any closer to the safety of the rock. She took out her phone and dialled 999. As she did, she made her way with her dog up the coastal bank.

'The coast guards are based nearby. I'm sure they'll be here soon. I'll run to the Brasserie and try and get help. Do something!' she shouted back to Ian.

Ian was suddenly alone again, watching his daughter exhausting herself splashing around in the blackening, icy cold water. The biting January wind was beginning to pick up again.

'Lucy, Lucy, hold on. I'm on my way down. Don't stop kicking your feet, just head for that rock!'

It was getting darker by the second. Lucy had finally managed the short distance to the rock, but the tenacious child was now struggling to hold onto its jagged edge in such cold water. Each chilling undulation was depleting her strength. On more than one occasion she had lost her grip, but the determined child hung on for her life for as long as she could. Ian knelt at the edge of the coastal path and grabbed hold of one of the upright beams that connected the railings. In a belated act of bravery, he lowered himself down to the steep coastal wall until his feet were touching the water and let go. The sharp, cold shock of entering the water made him shudder and gasp for breath.

Clinging on to the rugged wall, he glanced over his shoulder at Lucy. She was still just about managing to hold onto the rock, but now her head had gone under the water for the second time.

'Oh God, we're both going to die here if we don't get help soon,' Ian said to himself.

He moved away from the land in an attempt to get to his daughter. It was a futile act from a desperate man. Panic stricken, Ian splashed around in an erratic movement towards the rock before swallowing several mouthfuls of water. He had only succeeded in using up most of his strength, before drifting further from Lucy and the relative safety of the coastal bank. Now Lucy finally lost her grip, and the poor child went under for the third time. Her arms desperately waved around whilst the waves dragged her further from land and safety.

'Lucy!' Ian screamed, between swallowing down more gulps of the freezing water.

He was freezing, and hardly able to keep his head upright and out of the water. The sound of the coastguard's helicopter now became audible as it approached from the edge of the bay. Within seconds, the helicopter was hovering just above the rock. In the dying light, Ian could see that a lifeguard had begun making his descent down to rescue them.

Ian was now seriously struggling to get any words out.

'Please help us ... I'm begging you. I'm begging you,' he managed to cry out before a wave swept over his head.

The next thing Ian knew, he was lying beside his daughter on the small rock. They were both wrapped in foil emergency blankets. Coming to his senses, he heard a man's voice speaking to him.

'She's ok, but she's close to getting hypothermia. I'm going to get you both up to the chopper and straight to hospital.'

Ian shivered incessantly as he turned to Lucy.

'Lucy,' he said feebly. She was conscious, but exhausted and unable to respond to him. 'Thank God you're alive,' he whispered, before passing out.

His eyes opened. Slowly blinking, through his confusion he tried to make out the strange room he found himself in. A nurse stood by the window, pulling the blinds up to let in more winter sunlight.

'Mr Collins. You're finally awake.'

'I'm … I'm in a hospital?'

'Yes, Mount Neville Hospital. It's nearly eleven o'clock, Sunday morning, January 7 . The emergency services brought you and your daughter in last night.'

'Lucy...please tell me she's ok?' Ian asked as he struggled to move himself up in the bed.

'Yes, your daughter's ok. She woke about an hour ago. She's resting in a room down the hall. Your wife is in there with her. She's been in to see you a few times since last night. I'll tell her that you're conscious and quite coherent. Please try and rest. The doctor will be in to check on you soon.'

The nurse left Ian alone in the room. He was still in shock and exhausted from yesterday's harrowing experience.

Suddenly, Danni came into the room closely followed by a tall, wiry young male doctor with sandy buzz-cut hair.

'Ian, thank God you're both alive!' she cried as she grasped and kissed his hand.

She was visibly shaking, and her eyes were red sore from crying.

'Last night was just … hell.' She began weeping again.

Ian held his wife and began to sob.

'It was terrifying Danni … I didn't think we'd make it … I couldn't get to her … I couldn't save her … '

He tried his best to stay composed, but just broke down.

Danni clutched his hand tightly.

'You don't have to explain, you've been through enough. I'm just so relieved that you both survived. You need to rest.'

At that point, the doctor introduced himself. 'Hello Ian. I'm Doctor Brown. I know this was a very frightening experience for you Mr Collins, but your wife is right, you need to rest. We're going to keep you and Lucy in for a couple of days for observation.'

He had a quick glance at his notes before continuing.

'That young daughter of yours is one tough cookie. Apparently, she was taught Shock Response at school. It helps you control your breathing when the cold water affects your body temperature. That's one of the reasons she was able to stay in the water as long she did. Of course, you have the lady who called the emergency services, and more importantly the Coastguard, to thank for saving both your lives.'

Danni calmly walked over to Dr Brown.

'Doctor, I know he's only just coming around, but could I please bring someone in to see him? We did discuss it earlier. Please, just briefly. It would mean a lot.'

'Well, under the circumstances, yes alright. But, not for another hour or two. He really does need to rest.' The doctor turned to Ian, 'I will be in to see you later Mr Collins.' Then he left the room.

A couple of hours later, Danni came back to see Ian. He was sat up, awake, and staring out of the window. He appeared to be in a calmer state than earlier on.

'Ian, I know you're still very tired, but I really want you to meet someone. It's important.'

'Lucy … is she ok?" Ian asked.

'Yes, she's doing really well.'

Danni turned towards the door that she'd purposely left open.

'Come on. Please come in.'

A man in his mid-thirties entered the room. He was of a slight build, not much bigger than Danni herself in fact. He was dressed like a mountaineer, or a walker in his khaki fleece, dark grey camos, and chunky brown walking boots.

Ian stared at the man in consternation for around a minute.

'Mike ... Mikey Beynon ... is it?'

The figure before him looked so fit, healthy, and clean. Ian was understandably confused.

'I don't understand,' he said, turning to Danni. 'What ... what's he doing here?'

'It was Mike,' she replied. 'The Coastguard who got to you first. The one who got you both onto that rock and gave you the survival treatment before you were brought here.'

Ian now stared at them both in disbelief.

'Mikey ... you ... you were begging on the streets. How? You saved our lives.'

'I had help, Ian,' Mike spoke up. 'Someone was kind enough to help me, take me in. You remember that night I was attacked, outside the community café?'

Ian lowered his head in shame.

'Well I was attacked again not long after that in town. Anyway, Steve Llewellyn, the man who runs the café, he basically mentored me back to where I am now. Steve took me in when I couldn't find sheltered accommodation long enough to get back on my feet. You have Steve to thank for you and your daughter's lives as much as me. I'm training to be a paramedic again, and I volunteer with the coastguards as often as I can. When the crew got to the scene yesterday, I obviously got to your daughter first. It was a shock for me when I pulled you onto that rock and was able to see who you were for the first time.'

It took Ian a minute or two to digest the information.

'Thank you Mike. Thank you for saving our lives. That time up in St Joseph's … I'm sorry … I should have done something.'

'It's gone, Ian. We have to move on now. I just did what any decent person would have done. Like I say, I've been lucky. I was helped by a good man and given another chance. I'll leave you to rest now.'

As Mike made his way out, Danni stopped him gave him a hug.

'Thank you Mike. You're a good man.' She looked back at Ian, and then back at Mike before whispering to him, 'We're forever in your debt …'

THE END

BALL OF CONFUSION

'....people moving out, people moving in....vote for me and I'll set you free...Ball of Confusion, that's what the world is today..'

I remember hearing this song for the first time like it was yesterday. Fifty years ago, half a God damn century.

'...Segregation, determination, demonstration, integration,, evolution, revolution, gun control, sound of soul

shooting… Ball of Confusion, that's what the world is today..'

Yes, fifty years ago, and my Lord it's still a Ball of Confusion. Same today as it was then. I sit here, in this old armchair, in this shitty old apartment, listening to the same old records. I'm no armchair critic though. No, it's just old age. I'm an eighty-year-old man. Chest problems, heart disease. I can't go out there and get my voice heard like when I was younger. Back then, we got our news from the streets. Well, now I get my news from an Arabian news channel.

'….humiliation, aggravation, obligation to my nation….Ball of Confusion…'

Obligation to my nation? The greatest fighter that ever lived was treated like a criminal and incarcerated because he didn't want to fight a fraudulent white man's war.

Then forty years later, we had another bullshit war.

'...Eve of destruction, tax deduction.. people all over the world are shouting 'End the war' and the band played on… Ball of Confusion, that's what the world is today..'

Thirty minutes of news showing me thirty minutes of protests from all over the world. I'm watching kids protesting, governmental corruption in Iraq. A government my nation designed and created after more treachery and profiteering. Now I see riots in streets on this television that are less than five miles from where I sit. Another unarmed black man has been shot in the back by the police. Everything's on camera these days, and it still happens.

Look at these placards they're carrying. *'They kill us because they fear us!'* They're shouting, 'I can't breathe!' Brave kids. Strong people. They feared us back then too. They certainly feared Martin Luther King. That didn't silence us, just made us stronger, angrier, and more determined to stay brave. The only thing I fear is this damned pandemic.

'...saying Ball of Confusion, saying Ball of Confusion....'

Time to change the record. Jesus, I can hardly get out of this chair. There was a time when I could really move to that song! Let's see, what will we have next? Oh yeah, here it is, Gil Scott Heron. THE great American poet. Yep, without this guy the kids wouldn't have that nasty shit they listen to these days.

'...Did you hear what they said, did you hear what they said...they said, they shot

him in his head…a shot in the head to save his country, a shot in the head to save his country…Come on, come on, come on, come on this can't be real…'

That man was a prophet. He could drive a man to tears.

'…Find a shadow cast by rainbows, there you'll meet the sage…but peace won't be still of its own free will…'

Peace brother, peace. But as the great H. Rap Brown once said, 'violence is American as cherry pie!' No doubt about that. But you know I thought we'd have real change after 2008. Not just figureheads, empty statements and posturing. No, it's just the same old structure, same old wars, and the same old damned lies. That's all it is. We've got monsters in power. Yes Sir, they played their Trump card. It still makes my blood boil, watching these monsters in motion. Meant to be servants of the people. They're just servants to the rich and powerful. Now those monsters are richer than ever. It's that age old kinetic motion. Just keep pushing the same system, the same design. They're still using the same exhausted cogs to keep those wheels in motion. Those wheels racing past my window now. Damn sirens screeching, drowning out my tunes.

'....There will be no pictures of you and Willie Mae pushing that shopping cart down the block on the dead run or trying to slide that color TV into a stolen ambulance...the revolution will not be televised...'

'Race riot'. Those two words go so well together on the television and in the papers. I can see the mall's up in smoke again. It's been four days now. Four days of unrest. Oh no, I'm not condoning all this looting shit that's going on, but how are you supposed to control all that anger and rage? The media just zeros in on that to get the effect they want.

'...A rat done bit my sister Nell...with Whitey on the moon...her face and arms began to swell...and Whitey's on the moon...'

God, my heart bleeds. Just like in '67 and '68. All over the country again. From Florida to Boston, Houston to Wisconsin. I don't know, but these protests today seem more interracial though. I see whites, Asian Americans and Latinos in there. Maybe it's because these masks are covering most of their faces up? Hmm...reminds me of the Panthers.

'...I can't pay no doctor bill, but Whitey's on the moon...ten years from now I'll be payin' still...while Whitey's on the moon... the price of food is goin' up, an' as if all that shit wasn't enough...now Whitey's on the moon!'

Man, that mall is really going up in flames now. I can't sit here like this waiting for my home help. She's an hour late already. She won't get through this. Well, no curfew ever held me back. I may be old, but I'm not useless. I've still got a voice, and I'm gonna get heard! I ain't gonna wait until they find a vaccine, or before they put a white man on mars! Now where's that God damn mask...?

THE END

PIANO MAN

Sebastian Williams entered the record store with a confident stride. He was wearing his favourite Prince of Wales Check blazer jacket, black collarless shirt, and black canvas trousers. Matching black leather brogues and satchel completed the ensemble. He looked dashing, important even. It was nine thirty on a Friday morning in June. The store was empty apart from the assistant behind the counter. He looked like he'd just stepped off Quo's tour bus, with his tatty denim waistcoat and jeans, and a well-worn *Uriah Heep Rockin The States 74'* T-shirt. A badly outgrown Friar Tuck hairstyle completed the classic ageing hippy image of both contentment and denial.

After a cursory look through the store's classical CD collection - a paltry mix of 1970's *Hooked on Classics* and two Michael Ball LPs, - Seb made his way to the counter and presented his business card.

'Good morning Sir,' he said in his affected, cut-glass accent. 'My name is Sebastian Williams, Seb for short, and I'm a professional pianist. Classical pianist that is. Well, mainly classical. I do venture into modern jazz, and possibly Rag Time if and when it is requested. None of this pop and Rock-and-Roll nonsense of course. Although I have to admit, I do admire Freddie Mercury's early operatic dabblings. Would you mind awfully if I were to leave some of my cards with you, maybe place some in the window or by the counter?'

The store assistant picked up the card and squinted at the lettering for a moment before reading it out loud. His thick South Wales lilt accentuated each syllable.

'The Pee-arn-no-Maan … Seb Will-ee-ams. Right you are mate, looks good, fair doos. I like that picture of the piano in the spotlight, right next to your name. Classy. Amazing what they can do today, innit?'

'Indeed! These business cards certainly weren't cheap my dear fellow,' Seb replied. 'I had a hundred of them printed last week by a very reputable online company. Along with the new profile shots and the website, it cost me a bloody arm and a leg to be frank with you! If you look closer, you'll see that's actually an image of me playing my Kawai Novus Hybrid Grand piano on stage. It's the ebony custom version, imported from Japan, only fifty or so made. Oh, a wonderful night that was …' Seb's voice drifted off as he recalled in his mind the said concert.

The assistant's gruff voice brought Seb back to the present.

'Aye, it looks the bollocks, it do. I tell you what my boy, my Uncle Cliff was the closest thing they ever 'ad to an 'Ank Marvin around yere. He could make that bloody guitar talk, he could! And my old Grampy used to like his Bach and Vivaldi. It takes bloody years to play all that fancy stuff though son, don't it?'

Seb let out a condescending chuckle. 'Oh yes of course it does. Well, my credentials are also noted on my card if you care to take a closer look. BA, ArtDip, MMus, etc. I've recently moved back to the area after spending some years in the big city.'

'Cardiff?'

'No no, not Cardiff!' Seb answered with an irritated shake of the head. 'No my dear fellow. The Smoke. London. Would you care to listen to my latest recording?'

Seb began to fumble in the inside pocket of his blazer for his phone and a pair of headphones. The shop assistant began perusing the counter-top in earnest, before taking a large book from under the counter and made his way to the vinyl section.

'Nah ... well, I'm a ... I'm a bit busy at the moment mate. Stock taking and stuff. Got to look busy, butty! I tell you what I'll do though, my boss Mike, the owner of this place, he dabbles with bookings and that. He did an X Factor thing last year up The Workies.'

'Workies?' Seb inquired with a puzzled expression.

'Aye, The Workies. The Workingmen's Social Club, innit? Bloody big tin 'ut thing. All corrugated sheets it is. The kids on the estate burnt the old building down. Little bastards. They've got nothing else to do these days mind you. It's up on the 'ill before you get to Bont Las, next to the Catholic Church. You must 'ave 'eard of the Workie's mun!'

Seb screwed up his lips and slowly shook his head. He remained clueless as to the venue in question.

'Bloody packed out it was when they 'ad that contest. This duo won it, girl and a boy. Duw, she 'ad a hell of a pair of … uhh … anyway, I tell you what, Mike's cousin's got a nice bar in town. It 'asn't long been open. Supposed to have a cracking terrace bar an' all. I'm sure Mike said that they've got a piano up there. Aye, those terrace bars are all the go in the big towns and cities, so they say. Mind you, this one only overlooks the Job Centre and The Old Duke pub. What a shithole that is!' He laughed briefly. 'Yes, I'll pass your card on to 'im, son.'

'That could be an interesting proposition.', replied Seb with genuine enthusiasm. 'Yes, it could very well be a 'way in' if you like. An opportunity for me to perform, and for the locals to experience some high culture wouldn't you say?' His baby face lit up like a child who's just been given a surprise present.

'Gonna bring culture to the local populace are you son? ... to the masses? Well, good luck with that around yere!' the store assistant chortled.

'Everyone needs a touch of good fortune, my dear fellow, but it's hard work and determination that gets us to where we want to go. Good day to you sir!' And with that, Seb left the record store with a smile and a spring in his step.

'Mother, I'm back,' Seb called out from the hallway after arriving home later that day. 'I've just been speaking to a delightful man down at that record shop in the town centre.

A real character he was!'

Seb's mother Babs was sat at the table in the kitchen at the back of the small terraced house. She was on the phone to her friend Marjorie.

'I'm in here Stephen ... sorry ... Sebastian!' she shouted back, before quietly returning to her phone conversation.

'No Madge, he changed his name a while back, when he went off to college ... yes, well ... you remember, he always was different ... affected, you know. Things just got worse when his father died. The anxiety, and the outbursts. Ooh, he hated his old name. Do you remember? It was the kids at his old school. They used to call him Dr Strange, after that fella in the comic books ... the character's real name was Stephen Strange you see, and well, Stephen's ... sorry, Sebastian's always been a bit ... different you could say. Anyway, I've got to go, it sounds like he's back on his high horse again. So long, call you tomorrow.'

Seb walked through the lounge and into the kitchen. He took a seat opposite his mother at the table.

'Ah mother, I have some good news. I went into town earlier this morning for my uhh … meeting, and on my way I decided to pop into that record store. You know, the one opposite that large supermarket?'

'Yes, I know the one. It's been there since before you were born. Did you manage to sort out your benefits? You can't live on thin air you know, and I certainly can't afford to keep you. Not on my own, not with your father's passing. You're thirty years of age now, don't forget. You're not a kid any more. When I was your age …'

'Please mother, don't lecture me! If you just let me finish, I was getting to that point … it's about potential work!'

Babs sighed, and raised her eyes to the

ceiling.

'Is this actual work now, or another bloody airy-fairy scheme of yours? You're up to your bloody eyeballs in student loans, and you still haven't had any driving lessons!' she said, exasperated.

'You'll never understand me, my life and work. The Arts ... my raison d'être mother! Wasn't it Frederich Nietzshe himself who said, *'Sans la musique, la vie serait une erreur'*?

'Freddie Who?'

'God, sometimes I wonder if I'm adopted.' mumbled Seb.

'Now you watch your lip, young man!'

'Oh, but ambition, ambition can be so cruel...' Seb cried with his head in his hands.

'Don't start your bloody drama-queen nonsense with me today, lovely boy' Babs butted in angrily. 'I'm not in the mood for your *Liz Taylor going through the menopause* theatrics! You're following your aunty Fiona with your bloody highfalutin' talk … nonsense it is … and you used to put that accent on even before you went away to university. Bloody nonsense it is! Delusions of grandeur. All this living on people's floors and sofas when you were away, like some kind of tramp!'

'It's called couch-surfing mother. Lots of people do it these days.'

'Not at your bloody age they don't! Get your arse back to earth, and find a job … pronto! I know your father was partial to a good play now and then, and he liked his Mantovani recordings, but he was a grafter. He ran that opticians until he dropped …'

'Being a drunk didn't help,' Seb sneered.

'That's enough of it lovely boy! Don't disrespect your late father. He was under a lot of stress. Now, don't get me wrong, you always were a talented child. We were always very proud of you, even when you had your little ... uh ... meltdowns, and upset people, but we really wanted you to go into teaching ... to get a career, not chasing bloody pipe dreams into your thirties.'

'Teaching? Teaching?!' Seb cried from behind his hands. 'You know how I hated school, and anything that reminds me of being there! I lived for the reading groups, the drama and music performances, but everything else was a horrid ... '

Babs could see how irritated her son was becoming. She began to calm down a little, placed a comforting hand on her son's shoulder.

'Don't forget it was me and your father who paid for all those lessons ... piano, the harp, dance and what-not. Then I did my best to support you when you went away to study.'

Seb sat still with his head remaining in his hands. Then he gradually regained his composure. Sitting up straight, and pushing his lank strawberry-blonde hair out of his eyes, he quietly asked if he could continue to speak. Babs nodded her head and waved her hand at him impatiently.

'Well mother, I was about to tell you about a serendipitous encounter I had this morning at the record store with this charming gentleman … '

'Aw merciful Jesus, will you just get to the bloody point? Have you found work or not?'

'I am expecting a call very soon from the owner of the said store. Apparently, he's also a reputable agent and local talent scout, from what I can gather. It sounds as if they need a pianist for a newly refurbished terrace bar in the town centre.'

'A terrace bar, in this town? Are you sure?' Babs looked sceptical.

'Yes, it sounds quite nice too. Gentrification happens all over the place these days mother, not just in the cities, you know.'

'Hmm, well, I'd have to see that to believe it. Who's this businessman then?'

'A Mike something or other … oh, Mike Walters, that's it. I gave him the land line number, so I'll have to wait in.'

'Never heard of him. Why the land line, are you struggling to pay your phone bills again?'

Seb didn't answer. Instead, he picked up a recent copy of *Opera Now* magazine, and made his way into the lounge.

Later that evening, the phone rang at the Williams' home. Babs answered.

'Seb, Sebastian, it's the phone for you!' she called upstairs. Seb quickly made his way down to the hallway. 'It sounds like that agent bloke you were talking about.' Babs whispered as she handed the receiver to her son.

'Good evening, this is Sebastian Williams.'.

'Hello there. This is Mike Walters from Mike Walters Records and Mike Walters Entertainments Agency Ltd. I believe you were in my shop this morning chatting to Kev.' the coarse voice on the other side of the line sounded like it had smoked half of Cuba.

'Ah, good evening Mr Walters. Thank you for calling. Yes, I did have quite a charming conversation with him earlier today. I gave him my business card.'

'Yeah, he said they were well impressed son. So, I think we should get on with a bit of business ourselves then. Kev mentioned that you were interested in a piano gig at my cousin Mark's place in town. Be good to bring a bit of class into the town. Kev also mentioned Mark's just opened a nice terrace bar then? I believe they've also got a piano in the place.'

'Really? Oh, that's wonderful!'

'Yep, our Mark doesn't spare on anything. Especially down at Shakey's.'

'Shakey's?'

'Yeah, our Mark was a big Shakey fan when he was a kid. Shakin' Stevens. *Green Door* and all that malarkey. Listen, I know it's short notice, but Mark wants to get the ball rolling for Saturday evenings. Something different, someone like yourself. How does tomorrow sound?'

'Tomorrow night you say?'

'Well, that's if you're not already booked of course.'

' … uh … no, no, nothing booked as yet. Tomorrow night? Well then, I say *Carpe diem* Mr Walters!'

'Aw right, never mind then. You've got wrist trouble have you?'

'Wrist trouble? I'm sorry Mr Walters, but you've lost me now.'

'That thing you know, with the wrists

and all that....the carpel thingy. I know a lot of musicians get it.'

'…oh, you mean Carpal Tunnel!' Seb replied with a poorly disguised snigger. 'Ahem. No Sir, *Carpe Diem*, it's Latin. It means to seize the day … enjoy the present and all that … uh … malarkey as you might put it yourself! Tomorrow would be fine my good man. Now, there's the small question of my fee. We are talking business of course.'

'Ah, yeah, now … well, it'll have to be a trial run to begin with. I just want to see how you do with the crowd and the venue. You know, speculate to accumulate. I'll make sure you have a few drinks on the house. After tomorrow, I'm sure we'll be able to sort out some kind of arrangement.'

Seb hesitated for a moment while he gave some thought to the proposal.

'Well, I suppose business is business etcetera etcetera. A few drinks you say?

Well, I have been known for my sybaritic excesses from time to time! Ok then, tomorrow night it is.'

'Right, sorted. Be there for eight o' clock, and look sharp. Two forty-five minute sets it'll be, by the way. Ciao for now.' And with that, Mike Walters hung up.

Just then, Babs came into the hallway.

'Well, what's the news then? Did he offer you any work?' she asked eagerly.

'Yes, I will begin what will hopefully be a regular night of piano sessions at … uhh … Flakey's I think he said.'

'Shakey's, it's called Shakey's. Wake up dear.' Babs tutted. 'It's in the high street. That used to be a tidy area in my day. Doctors, Professors and what-not would socialise there. You'll have to get your head out of the clouds though Sebastian, it can get lively around there nowadays. Not exactly the Pavilion Tea Rooms.'

'Have some confidence in me mother.

I've performed in venues up and down the country!'

'I know dear, I know. Well, you just do your best. How much are they paying you by the way?'

'Umm, well … I won't be getting anything tomorrow night, just a couple of drinks.'

'Aw, I bloody knew it', snapped Babs. 'If this doesn't work out, you can get onto that teaching course. You promised me you would son. No more amateur dramatics … hanging around this house with all your thees and thous!'

Seb didn't respond. He just made his way back upstairs muttering under his breath about how nobody would stop him going back to 'treading the boards' if this venture didn't work out.

The following night, Seb arrived at Shakey's bar at precisely eight o'clock. As on the previous day, he'd decided to wear his favourite blazer jacket, black shirt and trousers. The obligatory black brogues and satchel were joined tonight by a black silk cravat. He certainly did stand out as some kind of artist.

He made his way up the main stairway and straight up to the third floor, where the terrace bar was situated. On arrival, his dashing appearance became all the more conspicuous alongside some of the regular clientele. A large group of twenty-somethings celebrating a birthday party looked like they'd turned up for a *Love Island* audition. Heavily tanned young men with arms like Popeye the Sailor, caroused with even more heavily tanned females, who were wearing next to nothing.

The bar itself was a pleasant enough setting though. A wall of glass doors and windows on the left led out to the terrace itself. A long bar ran along the right side of the room. Small circular tables with tub chairs were dotted around, along with a few old leather sofas. Pine panelled walls gave the room a retro, Scandinavian look. Seb was reasonably impressed. He headed to the bar and introduced himself.

'Good evening. I'm Sebastian Williams. I have been booked by Mike Walters Entertainments Agency to provide some piano entertainment here tonight.'

'No worries. Sound. The piano's over there butt, in the corner.' The bar tender pointed to the far end of the room. 'Start around nine. It should liven up by then.'

Seb glanced over to where the piano was standing. It was a tatty-looking upright, in what looked like a dark wood finish. He scrunched up his face in disdain, before turning back to the bar tender.

'Oh, just one thing,' said Seb. 'I believe there are a few drinks on the house for me tonight.'

The bar tender shrugged his shoulders and nodded.

'Well then, I'll have a large gin and tonic. No ice. By the way, is the proprietor in this evening?' Seb asked.

'Nah, he's in Benidorm with one of the barmaids,' replied the bar tender as he moved down the bar to serve a customer.

Seb took his drink and headed over to the piano. On closer inspection, Seb realised that the piano was an ancient 'Belarus' budget model from the 1930's. It had been given a recent coat of paint, probably by the bar tender. His heart sank. He lifted the lid of the piano. All the keys were there at least. After a little play, it was obvious that the instrument was slightly out of tune. Some of the higher keys were sticking too. Seb put his head in his hands for a few seconds, before quickly regaining his composure.

The terrace bar was getting busier. A group of casually dressed middle-aged couples filled a table near the bar. Seb began studying his sheet music. Getting the right choice of tunes was going to be very important for his opening night.

'Right, here we go,' he muttered to himself. 'Let's see now, a little Gershwin … Misty, by Errol Garner … Yes, I think that could work … some Scott Joplin … yes, definitely … ooh, Oscar Peterson's Night Train … now, I could be pushing the boat out, but maybe a Chopin prelude … surely they've seen *The Pianist*! He quickly scanned the crowd. One of the girls from the birthday party was hitting her friend over the head with a two-foot-long inflatable penis.

'Hmm … maybe not,' he said to himself.

One of the middle-aged ladies approached Seb with a request.

'Ooh, this is nice. I like a bit of piano and a sing song. Do you know any Celine Dion? *Don't Think*, that's my favourite!'

'Ah no, I don't I'm afraid. That's not really to my taste,' he replied with his trademark snigger.

'Oh right, fair enough then. Sorry to bother you' she said with a huff, before briskly walking back to her table.

Seb eventually began his first set after some hand-stretch exercises, and adjusting his cravat. The piano was an old dog to play, but he was warming up quite well. He even managed to avoid the few broken keys. The first three or four tunes went by relatively well. However, the crowd was taking very little notice of him. He was, after all, just something in the background.

Just then, a stag party dressed as superheroes stumbled into the terrace bar. They were clearly quite intoxicated, and very obnoxious. In fact, Seb thought that they made the *Love Island* crowd look like Young Conservative members. The ringleader, as wide as he was short, and dressed as The Incredible Hulk, instantly fixated on Seb and the piano.

'Fuckin' 'ell boys!' he shouted to his mates by the bar. 'It's fuckin' Liberace, look! Go on butt! Tinkle 'em ivories for us!'

Seb did his best not to allow this intrusion affect his playing, but he was beginning to sweat and shake a little. He could hear repeated shouts of 'Oy, little Lord Fauntleroy, play something we know, you posh twat!' coming from the direction of the bar. He was beginning to feel more and more anxious, and also very angry. His mind began to race. *If only they'd turned up later ... or not at all ... the buggers ... and this bloody piece of shit excuse for a piano ...on my very opening night ... this has been a big mistake ... these philistines ... it's like being back in school ...*'

The room was becoming increasingly rowdy, and the stag party was getting more and more unruly. Spider Man had managed to get hold of the large inflatable penis, and was simulating crude homoerotic sex acts with Ant-Man. In between drinking games, some of the party made frequent and prolonged visits to the toilets. They were usually in pairs, and noticeably sniffing like excited rabbits when they came back into the bar.

Still the barrage of taunts and insults towards Seb kept flowing. The hecklers, like all good pack animals, began to grow in numbers, and closed in on their prey.

'Oy, Oy ... Nancy boy!' one of them drunkenly ranted. 'See that scarf-thing? I'll wrap that around ewer fuckin' neck ... fuckin' Nancy boy!'

Seb was unable to cope. His playing was being drowned out by the mob. A seasoned performer, or a busker even, would have possessed a thicker skin. A pre-planned defence mechanism such as banter, or a witty retort, was alien to Sebastian Williams. It just happened that he was only half-way through Scott Joplin's famous piece The Entertainer when his playing really began to deteriorate with all the twitching and shaking, and from the sweat dripping into his eyes.

'Hey ... fuckin' 'ell boys!' the ringleader bellowed between fits of laughter. 'I thought Les Dawson was dead!' The whole crowd was now in hysterics.

Seb finally reached boiling point. He stood up from the piano stool and screamed his own stream of abuse back at the room,

'YOU MORONS! YOU'RE JUST LIKE SHEEP ... FUCKING SHEEPLE, THAT'S ALL YOU ARE! IT'S JUST LIKE SCHOOL ... DON'T YOU EVER GROW UP? FUCKING NEANDERTHALS! YOU

LOW LIFE MONSTERS AND WHORES!'

As Seb sat back behind the piano and attempted to play the famous intro to the Queen classic *The Seven Seas of Rye*, the ring-leader started to kick seven shades of shit out of him. Seb didn't feel the first punch, or even the second. It was a mixture of shock and adrenaline after the piano lid was slammed down on his right hand.

Cloisters Rest Home, a sprawling Victorian mansion set within two acres of landscaped gardens, was originally built in the late 1890s for the industrial magnates the Coleshays. Cloisters was advertised as, *'A privately run hospital and clinic...a perfect setting for calm, safety and peace of mind for both young people and adults with various mental health issues ...* ' The care was provided by *' ... well trained staff of the highest calibre...'* For the past week, it had become the temporary home of Seb

Williams.

Seb's room was quite spacious. White plastered ceilings topped eight foot high walls that were painted a calming primrose yellow. A small window looked onto one of the many beautifully landscaped lawns.

Seb sat quietly on the single bed, dressed in a pair of plain white pyjamas. He was staring at a television that wasn't turned on. He'd been heavily tranquillised since his voluntary sectioning. His jaw had been broken in the attack at the bar. It was noticeably bruised and swollen, but it was not considered bad enough to be wired up. He still found it very difficult and painful trying to speak. His right hand had also been broken. He looked pitiful, but the beating would have been a lot worse, had the bartender not called in the security guard from the ground floor when he did. His attacker hadn't been apprehended. Apparently there were three different Incredible Hulks out on the razz causing trouble in the area that night.

The hospital was expensive, and Babs had broken into her life savings in order for Seb to be able to stay there. She wanted the best care for her son as always. It didn't look as if Seb's recovery would be imminent. That meant that Bab's new car and Seb's prized Kawai grand would have to be sold.

Babs had just visited her son for the first time. She had always been a strong woman. She was also no stranger to Seb's histrionics and melodramatic outbursts, but it was still obviously distressing to see him in such a state. She was sat in the corridor not far from Seb's room, being consoled by a young nurse.

'It's happened before,' Babs told the young nurse quietly. 'Well, not this bad … but the tantrums, and the anxiety, when he was in school, and up in London … He has plenty of spirit, but he just loses control. He can't deal with stress, and he's always lived in a bubble. He was having therapy as a child. Megalomania some said, others thought it could be Attention Deficit Disorder. We had to take him out of school a couple of times. His father passing away when he was a teenager made matters worse. But he could be very critical and insensitive to others. Then of course he'd get picked on. We knew when he'd had trouble at school, because he'd put a sign on his bedroom door that said *'Persona non grata'*. I didn't even know what it bloody meant! Sometimes, he just couldn't keep his mouth shut … well, he hasn't got much choice now,' she said with a heavy sigh.

'Mrs Williams, I know this is obviously an upsetting time for you and Sebastian, but he'll get the care and rest that he needs here. I promise you.'

Babs left to make her way home, and the young nurse went back in to check on Seb. He was still sitting up in bed staring at the blank television screen. She came and stood next to the bed, and checked his chart, then looked at her watch. He had been given his medication just twenty minutes earlier.

'Hello Sebastian. I've just been chatting to your mum. She was telling me all about your musical talents. The Piano Man, I hear they call you. I've always wanted to play an instrument myself.'

Seb just groaned in response and raised his broken hand.

'Well once you get better and that hand of yours heals up, you'll be back wowing the crowds with your keyboard skills in no time. We can't let any set-backs get in the way now, can we dear?'

Seb shook his head. *'The Piano? The fucking piano?'* he thought to himself. *'That fucking thing has brought me nothing but pain and disappointment'!* He may have taken a fair beating, but his fragile mind still raged. *'You silly bint, nobody can vanquish the fire of my aspirations, the bold resolve of my character, and least of all, my unlimited creative potential! You clueless tart, it will be a return to the stage for Sebastian Williams, but this time, through stagecraft, performing arts, the ... theatre ... great ... greatness ... dest ...destiny ... '*

The medication had started to take effect. Seb pointed to himself with his left hand and did his best to mouth the things he wanted to say, but any attempt to move his jaw was very painful. He could only manage to utter one word repeatedly, and semi-coherently.

'Thespian' he said. 'Thespian ... Thespian ... Thespian ... ' over and over until the sedatives finally knocked him out.

The young nurse left the room and bumped into one of her male colleagues back in the corridor.

'How's the new arrival doing?' he asked her.

'Well, he's in for severe anxiety attacks. He's just had his medication, so he'll be asleep for a while at least. He was beaten up during a gig.'

'Yeah well, you've got to be careful these days, people crowd-surfing and stuff.'

'No, he wasn't in the audience, he's a pianist.'

'Oh Jesus, and a broken hand as well. Well, he won't be playing again for a while then!'

'No, he won't,' the young nurse said sadly. 'The physical and mental trauma is going to take its toll in the long term, no doubt. He was understandably very confused and in pain. Before he passed out, the poor thing just kept babbling on. It sounded like he was trying to tell me that he was a lesbian.'

THE END

BONNIE WOULD UNDERSTAND

The roads were quiet in the Wyoming countryside this time of day during midwinter. A black and chrome bus headed north on the long and straight Highway 90, having left Pittsburgh before dawn. Now it was close to noon, and the bus was only a half hour from its destination. It was freezing outside. The sky was split between murky white and dull grey clouds.

The bus was originally designed to carry fifty two passengers and one driver. On this journey though, only eleven people were on board. Inside the old bus it was almost as cold as outside. It had been built just after the Great Depression. An Art Deco-inspired relic from that harsh, unforgettable era. Now nearly thirty years later, it was ready for the scrap yard.

Thirty four year old Frank Kirby was sat on the left hand row of seats at the centre of the vehicle. A heavy-set man, weighing over 300 pounds and well over six feet tall, Frank needed the two seats for himself. His wavy, carrot coloured hair was neatly greased back. He was clean shaven and already dressed in uniform.

Frank sat perfectly still staring out at the surrounding countryside. The scenery they had passed through in this sprawling county had ranged from sparse and frosted plains to snow-capped mountains that towered over large, ice-blue lakes. His warm breath misted up the window, before he slowly wiped it clear again. He was oblivious to the other men sat around him. Most of them just muttered to themselves, while fidgeting and breathing into their hands to keep warm. Frank was in a warm place, or at least his mind was. It was 'mind over matter', that's what his mother said when he was a child. The bullying, the fights. His dad would just yell at him to quit his gibbering and defend himself. He didn't understand, but his mother would often tell him, *'If you think of what you want, of how you're going to get it, how things should be, then it'll turn out that way Frank. I promise you.'*.

The bullying had never stopped. Right through school, his teenage years, and in his workplace, the taunts followed him. *'Big Frankie-Stein'*, *'The ogre with the stammer'*, Frank Kirby took it all, but he always had that place to go to. In his mind he could make things right, make things how they should be.

Frank's mind now went back to the previous Christmas. He'd lost his job that December, the busiest month of the year for Boscov's department store. Frank still believed that he had been the victim of a witch hunt. His colleagues had informed management about his odd behaviour on several occasions that previous year. They said that warehouse workers shouldn't be hanging around the shop floors to begin with. They accused him of loitering near the store's foyer and wandering around the car park after his shifts had finished. Complaints were also made about Frank spending nights alone in the storerooms. When Frank explained that he wasn't ready to go home, no one would listen.

Frank was dismissed and denied a hearing by a court of law. A tribunal was out of the question, the employment unions were still weak in the state of Pennsylvania. Frank certainly wasn't capable of representing himself. No one was willing to represent Frank Kirby either.

He was hoping that Bonnie would understand. He was convinced she would. Frank felt that things hadn't been going well between them at that time either. The months leading up to his dismissal were particularly bad. Bonnie had barely made eye contact with him on the rare occasion that they did engage in any form of conversation. Frank would just shuffle awkwardly in front of her, mumbling and stuttering to himself most of the time. For so long now, he'd desperately tried to find the right words to tell her how much she meant to him. Frank was cursed by a hopeless, lifelong inability to express himself, and to express his feelings towards the people he loved.

The bus chugged past another large lake. Its dead calm waters perfectly reflected the clouds and the gigantic rock faces that dominated the skyline. Frank thought it looked like an upside down world. That's what his mother would say when he would come home after being bullied. *'It's an upside down world dear. A giant of a boy like you picked on because you're slower than those scrawny kids. They think you're weak, as harmless as a fly. They treat you badly, and people will always try to do that. You may be slow, but you're not stupid. One day someone's going to pay for messing you around!'*

Yes of course, Bonnie would understand. Frank was sure from the start that they would be soul mates, that they would always be lovers. He was still infatuated with her, but now she was saying how she preferred smaller guys. Then sure enough, she had started that stupid affair with the little accountant guy. It was an upside world alright. Yeah, but good old Frank kept his mouth shut. It was just that -

a fling. Bonnie was a teaser, not a heartbreaker. Frank knew that. Her and that Jimmy kid, it wasn't meant to be. She would finally understand that.

Frank could hear his mother's voice again. She'd passed away over twenty years ago, but her words of reassurance stayed with him. *'One day you'll find someone Frank,'* and *'She'll be the right one dear. You'll know. She may not be so sure at first, but you'll have to make it happen. Like I told you ... just think of what you want, then how you're going to get it.'*

The two women in his life, his mother and Bonnie. Bonnie had shown him great affection to begin with. She was the only woman apart from his mother who had ever shown Frank any affection throughout his life. Things had changed though. Before he'd lost his job, Bonnie had been saying how he was starting to give her the creeps. She had even told him that she didn't feel safe around him any more. Frank couldn't bring himself to ask her what he was doing wrong. As usual, Frank kept everything locked up inside.

She came home that Christmas Eve after last minute shopping to find Frank sat in the lounge. He gave her one hell of a shock. She dropped her shopping bags in fright. Just seeing him there like that, his huge naked frame hunched over dozens of photographs of her all over the floor.

'Jesus Christ ... how ... what the hell are you doing in here? Get out or I'm calling the police!' she yelled at him.

Frank looked up at her. There were tears in his eyes, streaming down his face. He was just as frightened as Bonnie. *Why doesn't she understand me ... what I'm trying to tell her. I still love you Bonnie.*

'I ... li ...live here ... now ... Bo ... Bonnie. I li ... live ... here ... now,' Frank managed to blurt out.

'God no! No you don't!' Bonnie screamed. 'Get out of here you crazy fucking monster!'

A man's hand grabbed hold of Frank's shoulder. The bus had reached its destination. Frank suddenly came back to the present.

'Time to wake up, you huge piece of shit,' the guard growled at him. 'Those better not be fucking tears in them eyes. I swear to almighty God, I'll smash this rifle butt over that stupid big pumpkin head of yours! We've reached Attica Correctional Facility. This will be your home for the rest of your sorry lives you sick fucking animals!' the guard shouted out, before turning his attention back to Frank.

'Well, are you going to get out of that seat and into line, or am I going to make you?' he barked while raising his rifle upwards. Frank got up as fast as he could, which wasn't very fast because his hands and feet were all chained together. He eventually got into the aisle and joined the other prisoners shuffling their way out of the bus.

Once outside, Frank and the rest of the prisoners lined up near the huge electric fence at the entrance of the maximum security jail. Flakes of snow gently fell on them and on the frozen ground. One of the other guards from the bus approached the one who had yelled at Frank.

'Woah, will you look at the size of that guy! What's his story anyway?'

'He threw a girl straight through her tenth storey apartment window on Christmas Eve. She landed face down on the side-walk.'

'That girl who worked at Boscov's in Philadelphia? That was all over the news.'

'Yeah. He worked there too. They worked together. He'd been stalking her for a while. Convinced himself that they were married, or a couple, or something or other. Lost his job because of it. He got into her place when she was out shopping. Must've put the fear of God into the poor kid, seeing that hulk there. He told the police afterwards that she would understand. Fucking fruitcake.'

THE END

Acknowledgements

I would like to thank all those, both friends and family, who read my drafts and have given me their honest feedback. Thank you, too, to my good friends Fiona and Gareth, who have encouraged and pushed me to finish this book, and especially to Fiona who has meticulously proof-read all of my stories.

As to influences on me, I must mention writers such as Guy De Maupassant, Ray Bradbury, Carson McCullers, Emile Zola, and Isaac Asimov. Their ability to put so much into relatively few pages has been an inspiration. TV shows such as The Twilight zone, The Dark Side and Black Mirror have given me something to aspire to, and having my own work adapted for the small screen is an ambition of mine.

Finally I would like to thank Alana Davies, who has edited this book and helped me put it together, and has reluctantly agreed to add her name to this page.

T.G. Hyde
April 2022

Printed in Great Britain
by Amazon